ISLAND SECRETS

R.S. Wolfe

ISLAND SECRETS

THE ISLAND ESCAPE SERIES, BOOK 1

R. T. WOLFE

ePublishingWorks!
love what you read.

Model photography by S.L. Jones Photography

Book and cover design by eBook Prep
www.ebookprep.com

July, 2019
ISBN: 978-1-64457-096-8

ePublishing Works!
644 Shrewsbury Commons Ave
Ste 249
Shrewsbury PA 17361
United States of America

www.epublishingworks.com
Phone: 866-846-5123

ACKNOWLEDGMENTS

Thank you, Suzi Fox and Glen & Claudia Wiseman, for your expertise with the authenticity of this novel and for your dedication to Anna Maria Island Turtle Watch and Shorebird Monitoring!

ONE

M ost divers perceived the sea as muffled, a world of regulated breaths and distant propellers. For Zoe Clearwater, complexity hid in the quiet. The ocean spoke a language few understood. To the animals here, every movement was an orchestra of life, each note revealing the exact size and location of creature waiting to flee or defend its territory.

This underwater world was both Zoe's heaven and her hell.

Hugging close to the Florida peninsula, she moved her fins ever so slightly along the sandy bottom of the Gulf of Mexico. The water caressed her face like a warm lover. It both soothed her aching heart and raised the hair on the back of her neck. Purposely, she followed the landmarks she'd detailed on her map. The freshwater caverns down the peninsula all looked similar to the tourists, but to her they were as different as the faces of her two sisters.

With an absence of the colorful fish found in the oceans, touring divers often avoided these caverns, generally preferring to explore the artificial reefs, shipwrecks, and larger caves. A number of wrecks had been sunk by Uncle Sam for this exact purpose. A few railroad cars were strategically placed and now provided habitat for fish, coral and visiting sea turtles. Some were clustered off the northern coast of Ibis Island, the place Zoe called home.

She dove alone today, something she regularly warned her scuba diving students never to do...back when she had diving students. Had her brother followed that rule two years ago, he would still be alive.

Swimming north, she passed one of the larger crystal springs caverns. She didn't bother exploring its depth. Seth wouldn't have gone in there. The smaller crevasses and openings were more his style. It was there, he'd convinced himself, that he would find Luciana Bezan's ancient dowry.

The wreck lay several miles out and was a favorite of the deeper divers. Legend had it, Luciana's lover ordered his best divers to escape with the jewels and trinkets just before his disapproving family sunk his ship. 'Let them search out there,' Seth would say. 'Divers during that era were trained well enough to swim great distances and hold their breath for insane lengths of time. My bet is that Luciana Bezan's lover ordered them to secure the dowry away from the ship.'

Zoe searched these smaller caverns just as she'd done nearly every week for the past two years. Seth had quickly learned to love the water. Who could blame him? Together, they had searched for the smallest, most hidden spots they could find, hoping to discover new, uncharted territory and possibly some ancient treasure.

As she approached a cluster of coral, she spotted an adult loggerhead. From the small tail, Zoe judged it to be female. She ached to follow her...see if she decided to break the rules and make her way up the beach to lay her eggs in broad daylight. Except Zoe had work to do, and she'd already been down here too long.

To her immediate right was the elongated cavern opening she and her siblings liked to call the palm tree, as it looked like a trunk with markings along the top mimicking palm leaves. To the south of her was the larger cave where tourists would be arriving right about then. She stopped at the smaller caverns she'd memorized, checking to see if Seth's fluorescent orange oxygen tank had washed in with the tide or gotten stuck between crevasses. Maybe the matching sack he always wore around his waist was hung up on a protruding rock. She would recognize them anywhere, even barnacle-covered after two years in the salty water.

A small tiger shark swam carelessly near, just as curious as she was. It was around three feet long and Zoe assumed had been fed by human hands at least once before as it came closer than natural for a tiger shark. She had nothing to offer and wasn't here to spend time with the wildlife. She was here for Seth. She owed him, and she owed her parents answers.

Thirty minutes of oxygen left. She would dive vertically, go in low, searching by sight and feel for any hidden caverns that might hide the remains of a thirty-five year old man or his gear. Then, she would get back to her boat. She may be stupid enough to dive alone, but she would at least return to the surface with air to spare. No need to risk taking another child from her mother and father.

Toward the sandy bottom was a cliff-looking structure with a breathtaking deep blue—almost black—base. Her fingers gripped the edge of the cliff just as rows of jagged teeth jutted out an inch from her hand. She froze both her feet and her fingers. Moray eel.

It came out further, this time exposing its yellow eyes and giving Zoe a once over. Instinct told her to flee, but she knew better. The mouth remained open as if it was speaking to her, its deranged eyes unreadable. Darting from its cover, the eel slithered to a crevasse below, fast enough to make her push out the breath she didn't know she was holding.

Heart pounding, she ducked beneath the underwater mound of protruding coral. She wiggled her fingers, thankful they were still there. The opening of the crevasse was the shape of a large baseball cap, hollow inside. Moving her blonde hair that floated like seaweed, she read the gauge that displayed the air level in her tank. Twenty minutes. Just one quick peek. After all, she had her reserve tank if needed. Then, she would record the spot and call it a day.

Inside was tight, no air pockets, and dark as night. She clicked on her flashlight, then moved the beam along the bumpy walls. There was no such cavern on any map she owned or had created. It must be hidden on regular days when the current churned particles and created underwater waves. A familiar tingle of excitement fizzled up her back. Seth would have understood. She might be the first to discover this spot.

No visible signs of life stirred. No fish, no plants. The walls looked like gray cumulous clouds scattered with deep juts every few inches. Since it was only about the size of a small kitchen table, she let her legs dangle from the opening below. Taking out her inadequate camera, she grinned, hoping Seth was playfully scoffing at the pitiful thing from somewhere above. She checked the settings, then clicked the first few shots.

Lifeless, empty eye sockets stared back at her on the digital screen.

She kicked and squirmed and screamed loud enough to nearly thrust the mouthpiece from her face. Her camera fell from her hands as she frantically worked to escape the tight area she shared with a human skull. She was stuck. No matter which way she jerked, her air tank wouldn't move. Keep your head. Keep your head. The more she panicked the more air she used.

Think. Be smart. She had thirty feet to rise. Releasing the

buckle that secured her air tank and reserve, she abandoned both and slipped away. With her breathing apparatus still in her mouth, she took one last breath before letting her diving weights fall to the floor below.

Maintaining a controlled ascent was nearly impossible. Calm. She forced her mind to the meditation her parents taught her from the time she was a little girl. She skipped both decompression stop zones, the image of a barnacle-crusted human skull burning holes in her mind.

It stared at her from the backs of her eyelids. Half a skull; she could see it clearly. Wait, her camera. She looked down and noticed it dangling from her forearm. She wouldn't look at the picture again. No need. It was etched in her mind regardless. Forehead, eye sockets. The complete top half of a skull and cheekbones. And a sea-battered knife sticking through one of the empty eyes.

Air. Her lungs demanded air. The ascent picked up speed as she neared the surface. It wasn't fast enough. Just one quick breath. She told her lungs to wait just another minute, but they wouldn't obey.

On the water's surface, Dane tried to ignore Zoe's boat, bobbing unmanned fifty yards from his own. Keeping an eye on Zoe was a nasty habit he could never quite break. Why the hell did she dive alone like this? The woman was like damned clockwork. Every Saturday. Walk her section of the beach on the west side of Ibis Island for signs of new sea turtle nests. Call in and mark any she found. Then, come out to this spot to search for signs of her brother.

Damn it, she'd been down there too long. He paced back and forth, his feet moving faster with each turn.

As the Sun Trips Touring captain, he was responsible for three pairs of divers that day. June tourist traffic was picking up. Considering his distraction with Zoe, it was fortunate all but one diver was experienced, and that one had a solid partner. The water was still that morning, and he could see them directly below through the emerald green.

He looked at his watch. "Damn it," he said out loud this time, then called out to his assistant as he toed off his shoes, "You're on, dude. I'll be starboard." He hoped the pitch of his voice didn't give away his concern. In one quick sweep, he both pulled his shirt over his head and threw on his air tank. Sitting on the edge of his mini-pier, he flipped backward, then swam as fast as he could.

College swim team felt longer than five years ago, and the flippers on his feet didn't make up for the drag from the tank on his back. He scanned the water top to bottom as he pumped his arms and legs. He spotted her just as she surfaced. Damned woman. He left his diving assistant alone with his tour group for this.

Lifting his head above water, he prepared to give her hell. But, something was wrong. She wasn't swimming toward the side of her boat. Instead, her body lifted awkwardly. She sucked in a gulp of air then choked out a lung full of water. Sprinting the last few yards, he grabbed her waist. Where the hell was her air tank?

She screamed and swung her open hand toward his head, kicking her legs wildly.

"Shit, Zoe. What the hell's the matter with you? It's me."

Her eyes were wild as she turned to him. He saw cold fear in them just before she rotated her head and vomited in the water. Ducking behind her, he crooned in her ear as he tucked an arm around her chest and swam both of them toward her boat. "Hey, hey. Babe. It's me. It's going to be all right." He suspected what she'd done. As soon as she was better, he would strangle her.

This wasn't his first rodeo. He'd owned his scuba business for years as a way to pay for his treasure hunting trips. He'd pulled in his share of stunned, dehydrated, and exhausted divers. Slipping off his tank, he plopped it on her pitiful protruding pier, then pushed it into her boat.

She was conscious but in shock. Too bad she wasn't the stick figure she'd been back in high school. It would have been easier to maneuver himself onto her pier and pull her in. The muscles in his body reflexively tensed as he recognized the faint shade of dark blue that tinted her fingers and lips.

"Hey." His hair dripped water on her face as he maneuvered over her and gave her a shake. "Zoe. What the hell? Are you okay?"

Her eyes rolled in his direction. She looked as if she'd seen a body. "Don't call me Babe," she croaked.

An unwanted smile spread across his face and, despite himself, he brushed the strands of hair from her smooth cheek. Checking the area, he spotted her pure oxygen tank under the boat dash. As he crawled to it, he noticed the expiration date was months away. At least she followed some rules. Her hand swatted him as he maneuvered the nosepiece under her nostrils.

"I feel fine," she whined.

"You won't soon. You ascended too quickly. I can tell. Breathe this, or you're going to feel it."

Of all things, she lifted her arm like she was checking for her frigging camera. Her lids closed when she spotted it on her arm. He hoped it was a sign of defeat as he slipped the oxygen tube around her head.

He glanced over his shoulder to make sure all was well with his boat, then searched for her cell in her bag. He couldn't leave his divers, and he couldn't leave Zoe. Knowing what he was doing, she grabbed his hand and shook her head. Cats' eyes the color of the green water pleaded with him.

"I've got a boat out, Zoe. How do you think I found you? I have six divers in the water. I can't leave them there with only my assistant."

She let go and her eyes drifted closed again. Life was much easier before she talked him into buying out her business, before she started working for him.

TWO

Dane called his best employee, Liam, and told him to get his ass out there. Liam reached the boats before the Coast Guard. Dane stayed until the EMTs took Zoe and long enough for Liam to get the divers headed back to the shop. He knew what she normally wore underneath her wet suit and what she had with her when the Coast Guard took her. One small bikini and her pocket-sized purse. He stuffed some of her things in a large, pink bag he found under the captain's chair, then drove her boat to the nearest public dock.

It took a good, long time to park the boat, let alone get a cab and learn which room she was in at the hospital. When he heard her sisters' voices, he almost turned around and left. The worry in his heart kept his feet moving.

He walked in to find, not only Zoe's sisters, but her mother and father as well, all standing around her. She sat fully upright on the bed with her legs dangling off the side. He couldn't decide if he was jealous of the camaraderie or thankful for being an only child with parents who lived in Alaska. The room quieted when he entered. Oh hell, he should have knocked.

"My bag!" Zoe said as if he'd brought her water in the desert. Relief coursed through his veins at the healthy color in her cheeks and strength in her voice.

Looking down at his arm, he gladly relinquished the bright pink bag.

"Hello, Dane," Raine groaned. "You can leave, now."

"Don't listen to Raine, dear. Come in, come in." Zoe's mother lifted from her chair. He adored this woman.

"Harmony." He lifted her hand and kissed her fingers. "You look as beautiful as ever." It wasn't a lie. Harmony Clearwater may have been in her mid-fifties, but she cared for herself inside and out.

Raine made a gagging sound as he turned his head to Zoe, who jumped off the bed and ripped off the hospital gown. She looked out of context in an emergency room with nothing on except her tiny swimsuit. Yep, he'd rather she was still the homely stick figure she was in high school. If so, his eyes might not have betrayed him as they stuck to her golden curves.

She tore open her bag and slipped her shorts over her suit. He wasn't the only one in the room who noticed the way she rubbed her elbows and knees as she finished with her t-shirt. Possible decompression sickness. Shit.

A nurse walked in at that moment and stopped her feet two steps before the rest of her. "What are you doing? And who let all you people back here?"

"I'm checking myself out," Zoe said as she slipped on her sandals. "If you need me to sign something, no problem. I have an emergency."

"An emergency bigger than the bends?" the nurse scoffed. "I'll have to talk to the doctor about this."

"It's been two hours. I don't have the bends, and if I do, it's slight. I can monitor my condition for the standard forty-eight hour period, but I'm leaving."

The nurse looked honestly dumbfounded. Dane, on the other hand, had seen Zoe do this before; the summer after her junior year in college when she sprained her ankle, the time she slipped on the deck of their business's pontoon boat and needed six stitches in her forearm. This couldn't possibly be the first time this nurse had a patient check herself out.

"Zoe, wait." Willow always was the peacekeeper. "You know better than any of us, you need to stay horizontal. Do it for Mom."

The glare Zoe gave her sister from the guilt-comment wasn't keeping any peace. She tossed the empty pink bag over her shoulder. "I need to get to the police chief. Dane, what did you drive?"

Mr. Clearwater spoke this time. Finally. A male voice of reason. "Zoe thinks she saw a dead body."

Dane's eyes shot to her, then to each of her family members as they stood in silence. They didn't believe her.

"It could be the bends fooling with her head," her mother added.

Zoe rolled her eyes and tapped her foot. "Do you have a car, or not?" she barked.

"I took a cab."

Without another word, she walked out of the room. It was curt, even for Zoe.

"Catch up with her, Henry," Mrs. Clearwater said to her husband. "She shouldn't be alone in her condition."

In her condition? Dane had to agree with Zoe on this one. She knew the symptoms and treatments for the bends better than all of them combined. Zoe was an excellent boat captain and had been an even better scuba instructor and guide. Obediently, Mr. Clearwater took off after her.

A dead body. Zoe shivered. She couldn't begin to imagine what kind of person might get themselves in a position to be murdered in a cave. Today, she was thankful her family lived a reserved life. Each held up to the family's reputation of simple, organic humanitarians.

The only thing worse than finding the skull of a murdered person was having everyone around you think you were hallucinating. She was without air for how long? Three minutes? Inwardly, she cringed remembering the panic she'd experienced. Outwardly, she rubbed her throat that still burned from the salt water. To be hallucinating, her ascent would've had to be longer and faster. Probably. And the aches in her joints could as easily be from the crappy day she'd had as they could from decompression sickness.

It was no use trying to ditch her father. He was more scared of her mother than he was of her. And Zoe did save a fortune riding in her father's car instead of taking a cab all the way from St. Pete's to Ibis Island. He hardly said a word on their drive to Ibis City Hall. He loved his family, his goats, his organic garden, and was the kindest, most patient man she'd ever known. Words, on the other hand, were not his thing.

City Hall was a single, small building. Zoe's dad walked with her through the only door along the front. The sensation was that of stepping into an elevator. Complete silence other than quiet music streaming from above. Zoe greeted the receptionist.

The tourist industry may be taking over the island, but it was still homey enough to come equipped with all the small-town features expected from an island this size. Right down to every-one-knows-everyone. She'd gone to high school with the receptionist and was surprised she didn't ask how Zoe was feeling. Then, she remembered only Dane and her family knew of her accident. That wouldn't last. It would take maybe two hours for the entire island to hear about the dead body.

"Good morning, Zoe, Mr. Clearwater. What brings you to our fine establishment?"

Zoe sensed cheap air freshener. Vanilla. And decided to bring fresh flowers the next time she came this way. "Good to see you, Glory. Gotta speak to Chief Roberts. I see his light on. I'll catch up with you later."

She dreaded talking to the chief—lazy good-for-nothing ass. He was on site the day her brother went missing. Every time she saw him, she swore he was judging her for leaving inexperienced Seth without a diving partner. As if she didn't already do that every day of her life. But she'd found a body; she had to report it.

They passed an office with a fake wooden nameplate that read, 'Mayor,' which must have hardly been used since the mayor was also the owner of the local supermarket. His office was next to a conference room with a paper meeting schedule taped to the door. The only date listed was the monthly town board meeting. A common area next to the offices held a handful of metal desks paired in twos. The chief's office was in back.

"Chief?" she called, walking through his open doorway. "I need to report a…well…a murder." The words sounded distant coming out of her mouth.

Slow as hell, his eyes lifted to her. "A murder on Ibis?" He said it as if it would be just as likely a Navy ship anchored at the Sun Trips Touring pier.

"No, no." As she sat in the far guest chair, she realized she might be in the wrong City Hall. What had she been thinking? She wasn't thinking. Her father slid into the chair next to her. Zoe looked around, trying to gather her thoughts. Stuffed bass lined an entire wall with fishing trophies beneath. The room was spotless. Not a pen out of place. The smell of artificial vanilla made her eyes water. "It happened just north of the caverns by St. Pete's. I found a skull, chief. A skull with a knife through its eye socket."

A sadness caught her off guard. A knife through its eye? What a terrifying end to someone's life. At that moment she decided to be a little extra thankful this *was* Ibis Island and not the busy St. Pete's.

"Now, Zoe, what are you talking about? A body decomposed enough to be just a skull wouldn't still have a knife stuck in it." The chief leaned back in his chair, his belly straining the buttons on his shirt.

That made sense, damn it. "I know what I saw."

He picked up a toothpick from his desk and stuck it in his mouth. "It's not my jurisdiction. Now, if you don't mind, I have work to do."

"That's it? Aren't you going to call the station whose juris-damn-diction it is? Give me a phone number? Anything?"

"If I did all that for all the people who came into my office, I'd have no time for the real work."

As if he ever had anyone come to him. Why bother? "I have proof." Her camera. Where was her camera?

"Dane," she growled.

Zoe found him in the gift shop side of the building that used to be hers. Now that she was just an employee and not the owner, she'd had more time to rearrange and redecorate. Scuba gear and equipment, pieces for snorkeling, shoes, swimsuits, and plenty of souvenir clothing and trinkets. Her air freshener wasn't artificial vanilla. It was the scent of clean salt water wafting in the open windows from the Gulf.

Of course, Dane's customer was young, blonde, and gorgeous. The way the woman laughed jiggling her fake boobs, Zoe almost suggested they get a room.

Dane wasn't much better. He used his looks for his benefit,

Zoe always knew that. It wouldn't have been so annoying if his looks weren't so…beneficial. His sun-kissed brown hair fell in lazy waves over his blue eyes and tanned face. He wore one of his Sun Trips Touring polos, exposing the barbed-wire tattoo that wound around his bicep and triceps. Turquoise beads lay across the middle of a thick, leather bracelet that matched the color of the shirt. Barf.

For the sake of the business, she would wait patiently, her father in tow, for him to finish with the customer. She was used to it.

Wait a minute. It wasn't her business anymore, or her customer. "Hey, boss," she called over the racks of scuba gear. "I'd like a word with you."

The look on his face made her smile. He always hated when she called him 'boss.' As he leaned in to say something in Bleach Blonde's ear, the girl looked as if he confessed that he ran over her cat. Ignoring Zoe, he walked to the back room, then came out with Liam who went for Bleach Blonde.

"Hello, Mr. Clearwater." Dane sauntered toward them as if Zoe wasn't there. "Let's talk in back."

"My camera, Dane." She followed the two of them to her former office. "Where is it?"

He looked to her father, then to her and must have decided on cordial. Sticking his hands in the pockets of his baggy khaki shorts, he answered, "I put anything that looked valuable in the storage box on your boat." From one of his pockets, he pulled out her keys and dangled them in front of her.

She bit her lip at the sight of them. She felt like a brat. "Thank you."

"And you didn't even choke on those two little words." He gestured over his shoulder where they kept their boats, personal and business. "I drove your boat back. It's in the dock."

Now, she really felt like a brat. "Thank you very much." She emphasized the very much, hoping it sounded sincere.

"You took a picture of the dead body?" He said it like he believed her.

"Yes. I'm going to go talk to the chief of police in whatever jurisdiction the palm tree cavern is in." She hated that he knew her well enough that he would recognize her personal reference to the cavern but forced herself to be grateful. "I'm pretty sure it's St. Pete's."

He looked to her father. "I can take her, sir."

Suck up.

"I was first on the scene. That is, after Zoe, here."

Her father seemed to consider for a moment before he nodded. "Harmony would be agreeable to that. And I believe her," he said to Dane as if it were an afterthought.

"You do?" she asked, honestly shocked. "Why didn't you say anything?"

He shrugged as he leaned down to kiss her on the cheek. "You seem to have it under control."

"I'm driving," Dane said before Zoe had a chance to call dibs.

They both owned Jeeps. Both were jacked with wide tires. Practical for trudging through the rainy season on a small island off the coast of Florida. Except Dane's had obnoxiously big tires, sat higher from the road, and was the same color as the turquoise polo. Each side, as well as the spare tire cover, advertised Sun Trips Touring.

He drove her the short way to the spot they kept their boats and walked with her along the weather worn dock. Like a gracious, appreciative woman, she didn't say a word about the privacy she craved. She stepped over the side of her boat, letting her sea legs catch up to the sway she'd caused. Dane followed.

Sure enough, all her valuables had been secured in her storage box. She took out her camera first and sat in the captain's chair. What if she did imagine it? She bit the side of her lip and glanced at Dane.

He lifted a brow.

She squinted at him and pushed the power button. Without letting herself stall another second, she chose the play feature.

And dropped the camera.

Her mind spun and wanted to sleep, but she forced her eyes open. The back of her head hurt like hell. Somehow she realized she was on her back, the hard floor of the boat beneath her.

"Damn it, woman. You need rest." He knelt over her. She smelled leather, and suntan lotion, and man. The soft corners of his face hardened and framed the cobalt blue of his eyes. Had she fallen? Warmth from his thighs brushed her waist. The muscles in them flexed and released against her slack body.

"Did you see it?" She tried to sit up, but he pushed her back down.

Reaching behind him, he grabbed a bottle of water. "You're not getting up unless you drink this. You've scared the shit out of me enough today."

"Okay, okay. You're right. I'm sorry, and thank you."

"Wow," he said as he released her shoulders. "Three thank yous and an I'm sorry, all in one day."

Rolling her eyes made her head hurt, but it was necessary. He held out her camera, and they rotated, sitting side-by-side.

Placing a hand over the screen, he said, "Drink first."

She waved the bottle back and forth, still in her brat mood, and took a drink. Propping her knees up, she rested the camera on the one closest to him. He leaned in as she pressed the play feature again.

"Whoa," he said as he stared.

The knife that was wedged through the eye socket of the skull, was surrounded by rocks and covered in crustaceans. It must be why it hadn't been swept away with the tide. Where was the rest of the body?

"Yeah, whoa."

THREE

D ane parked his Jeep and turned to Zoe. She sat rubbing her knees in the hot summer morning. Decompression sickness. It was no use lecturing her about getting rest, not until she got this over with. So, he pocketed his keys and slid to the asphalt. Gingerly, she stepped on his running board, then the parking lot. He had an urge to walk around and slide his arm over her shoulder, but he knew better. They weren't like that.

The St. Petersburg police department made the one on Ibis look like a corner drug store. Elevators, long hallways on both sides. Even on a Saturday afternoon, people walked around from room to room, trickling out of the elevators, and waiting in lobby chairs. He and Zoe stopped at the reception counter and, surprisingly, she let him do the talking. "We'd like to report a…crime."

Zoe jerked her head to him. The woman was an endless mystery. He read the frustration in her eyes but had no clue about the cause.

"What kind of a crime, sir?" The receptionist was a man and wore a crisp uniform. He seemed young enough to be in high school.

Dane looked to Zoe who was still staring at him. "The lady, here, found a skull stuck in a cavern. With a, uh, knife, ya know...in it."

"Fill out this form, and wait over there, please." The dude gestured to a row of glossy chairs along a far wall.

They sat in the chairs as he started filling in her information. He leaned into her as he asked the questions he didn't know the answers to. There weren't many of them. The smell of clean salt water filled his senses as he realized she wasn't pulling away from him. Her answers were methodical without a single word of sarcasm. It was all freaking him out. "Babe. Are you okay?" he asked as he wrote.

"I don't feel so good."

She didn't give him shit for calling her, 'Babe.' "Are you going to puke again?"

"I puked?" She looked around the ceiling like she was considering before she shook her head.

"Pass out?"

"No. I'm fine. Let's do this. I captain the party boat tonight."

"Yeah, right. I can read the headlines now. Woman with the Bends Crashes Sun Trips Touring Boat. I'll send Liam."

"It's his day off."

"Are you sure? He came out this morning when I saved your life."

"You did not—"

A man dressed in a button-down shirt creased with a holster came from the hallway on the right. "Good day. I'm Detective Osborne. Are you the two who have a crime to report?" He held out his hand. Dane took it and shook.

"We do, yes. I'm Dane Corbin and this is my—"

"Employee," Zoe interrupted stepping forward.

"Very well." The detective took the clipboard from Dane's hand. "Let's head upstairs, and we'll see what you've got." He glanced through the papers on the clipboard as he walked toward the elevators.

Dane rested his hand on the lower half of Zoe's back as they followed. The office was small with wooden mini-blinds that were pulled closed. Dane gestured for Zoe to sit, then he followed.

"So, it looks like you have…" Osborne trailed off as he read. He must have gotten to the knife through the skull part, because his eyes turned to them with brows lifted high.

Zoe pulled out her camera. "I was diving due north of the cavern just west of town." As she turned the camera on, Osborne stood and thumbed through a file cabinet. He returned with a map just as Zoe held out the camera. "I discovered a crevasse. In it, I found this."

Osborne eyed the photo, then opened an underwater map of the area. "Can you pinpoint the location? We can get a crew down there ASAP."

Her beautiful green eyes grew as she ran them over the detail of the map. Dane knew what she was thinking. She'd never moved on from the death of her brother. It was why she came to him more than a year ago, crying in his office. She wanted to sell her scuba diving business, merging it with his. She didn't want it anymore; didn't feel qualified to be in charge of divers…of people.

They'd never been close, he and Zoe. Grown up together, sure. Fooled around once in high school—which her sister would never let him live down. But the day Zoe came to him; he didn't even consider. He agreed to buy her out flat on the spot. Since then she'd been filling his mind with ridiculous thoughts and ideas. He followed her nearly every Saturday, keeping an eye on her as she dove searching for signs of her missing brother. Dane ought to be out on the Pacific, looking for his next haul of treasure. Yes. He knew what she was thinking. Her mind mesmerized the detail of Osborne's map.

No, he should be here.

She still led party pontoon expeditions and captained the snorkeling and bird sanctuary tour. Even manned the gift shop. But she hadn't taken out a single scuba group since the day her brother died. He let his lungs fill before he exhaled slowly.

"Can I take some pictures of this?" she asked but didn't wait for an answer.

The detective looked surprised as Zoe clicked off shots of his map. Dane wanted to tell him to get used to her forwardness. He had.

"Where did you say you found the skull?"

She pointed to an area near the bottom of the coastal wall.

Osborne dipped his head closer to the map as Zoe clicked off another dozen photos. "There's nothing here, miss."

It was the first smile he'd seen on her face since he pulled her out of the water. It knocked him off balance like it always did. She may have been gangly back when they were in high school, but her smile could always change the pull of gravity. He would never tell *her* that.

"It's a bit of an optical illusion down there, I'll admit. Send your guys. They'll find it." She started to get up.

Osborne placed a hand on her forearm. She looked down at it, then up at him.

"I still need a statement, miss. And I'll…need that camera."

"What? I just took eighteen pictures."

"You'll get it back, but it looks like a person might have been killed. Maybe we should give him or her priority." Dane found himself impressed with the way Osborne put Zoe in her place without putting her in her place.

Dane waited patiently as she gave her statement. Three times. Then, they asked him about his involvement. Twice. They were there for over an hour. If this really was Liam's day off—and Zoe never seemed to be wrong about these things—Dane would be pushing his luck asking him to captain the party boat. Maybe he would just do it himself.

"Keep my camera?" Zoe moaned as she tilted Dane's bucket seat back as far as it would go. "They're going to have to keep my camera?"

"Murdered person." Dane was just rubbing it in, she knew. He plugged in his Smartphone and started up his reggae playlist.

It's not like she didn't care about the dead person. She reported it, didn't she? Twice. "I just don't see why they couldn't upload the pictures and give me my camera back."

As he drove, she turned her eyes to the sky. There was nothing quite like a clear, blue Florida sky. The island breeze cleared her thoughts. She let her lungs suck in the air and her eyelids drop. The scenario reminded her of Seth. He was ten years older and generally the one in charge of driving her and her sisters around the island until he was old enough to move away and go to college.

Her parents loved them dearly. She knew this. But the minute each of them turned eighteen, their bedrooms suddenly turned into offices and craft rooms. Either go to college or get a job. 'It's your choice,' her mother would say with a warm smile. The corners of Zoe's mouth lifted as she dozed off.

In her half-conscious state, turtles drifted near her in the sea grasses. Seth tapped her on the shoulder, then jabbed a pointed finger at a new cavern he'd discovered.

She swam uncomfortably near it. She was never uncomfortable diving with Seth, but she didn't want to see in this cavern. He grabbed her wrist and pulled her toward it. Why was he doing that? He grinned as he gestured inside. Obediently, she lifted her head. Her legs started to kick as she spotted the skull.

Seth held his tight grip on her arm. Her eyes locked on an enormous skull that stared at her. Two large moray eels darted at her, one from each eye socket.

It was either the terrifying image or the familiar feel of the hump in her parents' drive that startled her awake. Was she driving? Riding with Liam? Bolting to a sitting position, her head spun enough for her to grab the side of it like that might keep it from falling off. She leaned back against the reclined seat as she remembered she was in Dane's Jeep.

Wait a minute. With a fear of head spins, she stayed semi-horizontal and turned her head to him. "You didn't dare take me——"

"Damn right I did. This is the second and a half time today you've passed out on me. I called the boss."

She knew who he meant, and it was a mean trick. Her mother was a vegan, belonged to a number of conservation groups. She taught Zoe, Seth, and their sisters how to meditate and use organic herbs for relaxation. She could also turn into a mother grizzly bear when her children were threatened. Dane had gone behind Zoe's back. It wasn't the first time.

"What do you mean second and a half, you traitor? I only passed out once today."

"There was the time when you looked at the picture of the dead dude—very cool shot, by the way—again, just now in my Jeep, and I'm counting when you were in shock from the bends as a half. You did nearly puke on me."

"I wasn't in shock. And I was resting my eyes just now. I didn't pass out. Are you sure I puked?" She still didn't remember that part and knew he would make it up if it suited him.

At that moment, her mother stormed out of her house. "Oh shit," Zoe said softly, then hit Dane soundly in the arm with the back of her hand. "What the hell did you tell her?" she asked out of the corner of her mouth.

"The truth," he said through his teeth as he smiled at her approaching mother.

It was an opposing sight. Herbs dripped from planter boxes that lined the front porch rail. Sunflowers towered over the porch and hollyhocks lined the drive. This year, Zoe's stucco childhood home was painted bright yellow and covered with her mother's latest artwork. Larger-than-life goldfish swam around a ginormous mermaid. All of it topped with her father's four female goats that grazed on the thatch growing from the roof.

The opposing part was the way her mother marched like General Patton's right-hand-man toward Dane's Jeep. Zoe was too scared to laugh.

"A grown woman and look at you," her mother barked. "You've got us all worried sick. I've got your bed ready and tea brewing." She put up a finger and nearly poked Zoe in the chest before she could say a word.

Instead, Zoe took the easy target and mouthed to Dane, 'I'll get you for this,' before taking her mother's outstretched hand.

Forty-eight hours. She could do this for forty-eight hours— the period of time symptoms could appear or worsen if one happened to have the bends. Which she did not. Thirty-six hours, really, since it was afternoon already.

"Half the town has called asking me how you're doing."

Half the town? How did they know already? Oh right, small island. The house was open with a warm breeze that ruffled the pastel orange curtains of the cozy living room. Her father sat reading *The Great Gatsby* in his ancient recliner. "Hi, Dad. Long time no see." Semi-retirement looked good on him. The restaurant they owned seemed to do okay without their constant presence.

Eyes matching the sea green color of her own smiled before her father took a sip from his flower power mug and returned to his book. Her mother led her down the short hallway with walls covered in family photographs. Homemade artwork filled the spots between photos of Zoe, Seth and their sisters. Shells clustered into the shapes of the seashore birds that gave Ibis Island its name. Some frames contained depictions of the endangered sea turtles their family had taken under their wing to protect. The ancient hardwood floor creaked as they made their way to her old room.

The only things that remained the same here were the smell of clean linens and fresh herbs. Well, that and the lines of beads that acted as the door. They still hung in thin columns providing pitiful privacy. She lost door privileges the night she snuck out of the house to neck with Roy 'Renegade' Cooper her junior year of high school. Willow had been none too happy about it since they shared a room growing up.

To go along with the move-out-when-you're-eighteen rule, her parents had transformed it into a den the summer Zoe left for UF. It was now fully equipped with a desk and futon. The futon had already been opened and covered in organic sheets, a blanket, and two hypoallergenic pillows. Bed or no bed, the smell of lavender incense told her she was home.

"You're quiet," her mother said as she turned down the covers.

"Just thinking."

"When he called, Dane told me the skull you found was murdered."

It made her laugh. "I'm not sure if a skull can be murdered, but yes, I found a skull belonging to a person who was definitely murdered."

"I'm sorry I didn't believe you."

Zoe turned to look at her. The lines on her mother's face had deepened since Seth's disappearance. Zoe knew she never quite accepted his death. She couldn't call her mother's actions denial, but something wasn't right. She barely spent any time in the restaurant anymore.

Her mother was a beautiful woman. Blue eyes and long, blonde hair streaked with the gray that made her look even smarter than she already was. As she generally did, she wore it in a youthful ponytail exposing her golden skin and cheerful oval face.

They spoke of Willow's bar and the latest antics of Willow's daughter, Chloe. Conversation changed to the restaurant, then to Raine's obsession with the island's marine conservation efforts. Of Seth, and how they hoped he was swimming in the sea in the sky with loggerheads and surrounded by the treasure he always wanted to find. And they spoke of the family belonging to the person who got himself or herself caught up in a death so violent it was made for the movies. She hoped the family would soon find closure.

"Do you think it was…" her mother said barely loud enough for Zoe to hear.

"No, mom. It couldn't be. The layers of crustaceans on that thing mean it's been down there much longer than Seth. And how could a Clearwater get mixed up in a murder? I love you, but I'm not happy that you listened to Dane Corbin of all people. You know he's a manipulator. A manipulator and playboy."

"Things are rarely as they appear, dear. He's just a boy."

"He's a twenty-seven-year-old man," Zoe retorted.

Her mother sat cross-legged next to her on the futon, sipping something that smelled fruity. Definitely not the chamomile that was in Zoe's cup. Obviously using the mug to hide the fact she was smiling, her mother mumbled, "You're still angry that he tricked you into second base under the bleachers your freshman year. It's perfectly natural to be embarrassed, dear. You weren't as…developed back then."

"Oh yeah, well I was perky," Zoe said in defense. "And I was a sophomore. I had perky little sophomore breasts and Dane Corbin should be glad I let him trick me—manipulate me—into showing them to him. I was lucky Raine showed up when she did. She nearly kicked his ass. And now I have bigger, perky breasts." She sat up straighter and held one in each hand as they laughed together.

She and her mother turned their heads to the knock on the doorframe, then jingle of beads.

A smile the size of the mermaid on the side of the house spread across her mother's face. Zoe could have crawled in a hole and died.

"Size matters." Dane grinned as he walked in carrying the oxygen tank from Zoe's boat.

FOUR

Zoe would slap him the first chance she got. "You wish you knew," she growled.

"True." Dane turned to her mother. "She should wear this while she sleeps. Or at least twenty minutes every few hours since I don't know if she'll get much sleep."

"Don't you have a business to run?" Zoe interrupted, her aggressive tone completely justified.

"It's Greg's day at the gift shop. Lilly is checking in tourists and both the party boat and the three snorkeling/eco tours are captained. We have no scuba groups until tomorrow afternoon."

"I needed the money from this weekend, Dane. You're costing me."

"Use your sick days."

"I don't have sick days."

"You do now. Babe, I'm the boss."

Sick days? She tried to protest. Wanted to argue that the other employees already thought she was sleeping with him. Why else would he have agreed to merge their businesses? Leaving him little time for the treasure hunting trips he was known for?

Now, she was given sick days? But it wasn't her business anymore. It pained her as much as it relieved.

"I can't sleep with the noise of that machine, Mom. I'll wear it later. Right now, I'm going to finish this disgusting tea and catch up on email. You have one night. Both of you." She pointed a finger from her mother to Dane. "I have Ultimate Frisbee tomorrow at two."

They looked at each other and spoke some silent language. The nerve.

"I've been wanting to crash Sunday Ultimate Frisbee for years," Dane said as he winked at her mother, then turned to Zoe. "I'm taking your place."

"You," she said flatly. "Can you even throw a Frisbee? Do you know how to play?"

"Look at me." He gestured the backs of his hands from his shoulders to his hips. "I can't look like this and not know how to throw a Frisbee."

"Arrogant—"

"Careful, babe. Your mother's here. It's like rugby, right?"

"You don't even know the rules." Although, *she* knew he would be good, great maybe. Would her team want her back? "How many steps can you take when you have the Frisbee?"

He squinted at her before he answered. "None."

Arrogant mind reader.

"Look, Zoe. This is serious. Use your head. I'm outta here." He kissed her mother on the forehead. "I'm sorry about the scene, Harmony. Your home is as lovely as ever."

"You should thank Dane for going to the trouble of bringing your tank for you, dear." It may have sounded like a suggestion, but it wasn't.

"Thanks, *boss.*"

Now, all Dane could think about was Zoe's perky A cups. Imagining high school A cups gave him the creeps. Yet, there they were, right in his face.

He had to drive all the way inland because the only drugstore on Ibis Island didn't carry extended oxygen tubes. 'Can't sleep with the noise of the machine.' She was the most high-maintenance, independent, fascinating, low-maintenance woman he'd ever known.

An image of her sleeping with those damned adult B cups—possibly C cups—rising and falling soundly kept his foot on the gas all the way to the inland store. And he had to captain her party boat that night. It was Liam's day off. A fact he would have had no trouble ignoring if Zoe hadn't pointed it out. She was going to make him insane.

He parked in the farthest spot of the drugstore lot. Zoe liked to call it new-car-parking and relentlessly teased him about pampering his jeep. He was simply taking care of his vehicle. She was a woman. She wouldn't understand.

Also in the figurative new-car-parking section was one black Beemer convertible. He wondered who it could belong to. Not. Richard Beckett was the island's richest, most successful jackass realtor. He cared only about his and his own and gave no respect to the sea turtles. That kind of thing didn't set well with a family like the Clearwaters.

Beckett came out in his Italian shoes, pants and matching linen shirt. He slid his $300 sunglasses over his eyes and ran his hand through his $80 haircut. "Dane!" Beckett said with a salesman smile. Must play nice with the locals.

"Hey Beckett. What brings you out in this heat?"

"It is a warm one." Beckett held out his hand.

Dane shook like a gentleman. "I see you bought the place next to my shop. Welcome to the neighborhood," he lied and realized he had no idea what Beckett wanted with the area.

"I've got a bid on the property next to it, too." His face fell as if he'd just realized he was forgetting something important. "Don't mention anything to your new employee, will you?" he whispered as if anyone could possibly hear him. "No need to stir the pot over nothing."

He assumed he meant Zoe but wasn't sure what pot he would be referring to. They said their empty well wishes and Beckett spun out in his BMW. Dane couldn't help it, he glanced down at his clothes and decided it might be time to grow up.

Zoe's eyes flew open. The moon cast stripes of light on the desk at the opposite side of the room. She'd heard a crack. It was the dream she'd been having. The skull stared at her as she lay on her parents' futon. The knife had turned itself just enough to crack the thing open, spilling pieces of Luciana Bezan's dowry between the barnacle-infested bones. Sparkling necklaces and silver flatware slithered out like the Moray eels of her last dream.

Freaking scary.

She knew her way around the room enough to keep the lights off, but with the creepy dream and creepier noise, her fingers ached to turn on the bedside lamp. She was no wimpy girl and instead forced her hands into the pockets of the sweat pants she wore to bed before standing and shaking her head clear. Clearwater's were not scared of the dark.

The extended oxygen tube Dane had brought her made it all the way to the bathroom. She pulled the thing off her face and set it on her pillow.

The digital clock on the desk read 2 a.m. She would get herself some of the raspberry decaf tea her mother had been drinking the night before, not any of the chamomile crap. Maybe she would read some news on her Smartphone, then get back to sleep. Although shivering another post-dream aftershock, she forced herself to stay away from the light switches.

The only bedroom in the house that acted as a bedroom was her parents'. She guessed when all of your children—all of your living children—resided on an island ten miles long, it wasn't necessary to keep guest rooms. She passed Raine's old room on the way to the kitchen. Raine and Seth were the oldest and had had their own bedrooms. Raine's was now a craft room and Seth's a music room with wall-to-wall string and wind instruments. Two banjos, Willow's old cello, an acoustic guitar, and an ancient accordion with marble keys.

It made her nearly forget about the dream and the tea. She wandered the room as the light of the moon forced its way through the paper-thin blinds. Propped in a corner were a few of Seth's things. It was worse than if her mother had been one of those parents who kept their dead child's bedroom exactly as it had been. Because he had no bedroom. No place. No house. No widow. No children. Nothing but the wide-open water somewhere in the sky Zoe hoped he was diving in right at that moment.

His wooden chest rested in the corner closet. Her mother refused to open it. She told everyone Seth wasn't in his dresser. His soul had moved on. One of those eccentric ways her mother had about her. Zoe was used to the odd antics. As a young woman, Zoe grew to adore and sometimes admire them. Now, she thought her mother was full of shit. She was stuffing her grief and avoiding closure. As if Zoe had room to judge. She was still looking for her dead brother in random caves every Saturday.

The dresser he owned stood as guard of the closet. It was odd the closet door was open. Her mother may be cluttered and eccentric, but she was tidy. Zoe's eyes had adjusted to the dark enough to see the scratches in the worn fronts of the drawers... that had also been left open?

Shadows from tree branches blowing in the wind were strangely alive. It was the dream, that was all. Regardless, some light seemed like a necessity after all. As she headed for the switch by the door, one of the shadows followed her. It grew and sprouted on a front wall, the moonlight giving away the form of a man. Too frightened to turn and see, she took off for the open doorway in a silent panic. But the man was faster. He covered her already speechless mouth with his hand and wrapped his other arm around her neck. How? Her brain spun in a worthless mass of fear and confusion. Why?

His arm flexed and squeezed her neck, closing off her air. She didn't think. Her fear reacted for her. Twisting like a mad woman, she dug her elbows in his ribs, right then left, again and again. He let go enough for her to scream, scream at the top of her lungs.

The man shoved her aside, sending her toppling over Willow's cello. She squirmed as if she had bugs crawling over her skin, trying to escape the instrument and to find a light, her parents, a phone, an escape. The front door opened, but she didn't hear it close.

What she did hear were footsteps running from the back of the house. Her father's deep voice never sounded so frightened or so beautiful. "Zoe? Where are you?"

"I'm in here," she croaked, rubbing the sides of her neck as she rolled free of the broken instrument.

The lights flew on and her father stood checking her from head to toe. Her mother followed closely behind. He seemed to be analyzing if she was really hurt or whether he could chew on her for breaking Willow's old cello.

Not ready to try her legs, Zoe whispered, "A man. There was a man. A man was in here. He tried to choke me. I screamed, and he ran." Saying it out loud made it all the more real and tears started streaming down her cheeks. The smell of over-bearing musk cologne stuck in her nostrils.

"What? Oh my gosh, Zoe." Her mother sat on the floor next to her as her father picked up her tossed phone. He headed for the front of the house, turning on lights as he went. The light was a welcome wave of warmth and helped her breathe steady enough to tell her mother the whole story.

In repeating what happened, and again to the police, she realized the man was smaller than she imagined in her petrified state. Not short, but a small build. Could have been a teenager. Probably was, the idiot. He broke into a house full of people. A house with nothing anyone would find of value. Her parents weren't into electronics or expensive jewelry. Unless the thief planned to find a seller for a steel guitar, a ukulele, or some seashell necklaces. What a hell of a weekend.

"Watch your step and your head. Welcome aboard the newest Sun Trips Touring vessel. We'll depart shortly." It wasn't a lie. This was Dane's newest pontoon. Zoe sat contentedly in the captain's chair checking the instruments. He had it painted in his signature turquoise blue with emerald green waves on the sides of the boat and a bright yellow sun along the canopy. The business had taken off since the merger—or since she turned her shop over to him. It was difficult to think of it that way, but it had all been necessary.

Chairs lined the sides under the canopy with a few more in the bow. She had two coolers, one in the front and one in back, stocked with bottles of water and sports drinks. The extra waste can for recycling was a personal addition of hers.

The business was part of what killed her brother. She had been so wrapped up in Sun Trips she forgot about her family, left behind anything resembling a love life, and left her inexperienced brother without a diving partner. He died alone. Never again would she captain a scuba dive.

A recent habit she picked up, Zoe rubbed the sides of her neck as if they still hurt from the attack. Could one of these customers be the one who broke into her parents' home? It was a question she silently asked herself during each tour she captained.

"My name is Zoe Clearwater, and I'll be leading your tour today. Please feel free to sit anywhere. There's room up front if you'd like some sun." Ten passengers on both her morning and afternoon tours. Capacity. She scanned the faces of each man, memorizing them. Judging their size, their build.

"Please take notice of the life jackets, ring, and fire extinguisher. You don't need to know how to use them, just where they're located. Thank you. We're going to stroll out, first to a favorite spot the dolphins like to play at this time of day. Please ask any questions you think of. I'm here to help."

The lull of the engine was therapy. It soothed her as much as she was convinced it did for the tourists as well. Although brilliantly sunny, the wind was breezy, the water choppy. The clean air refreshed her face. She dipped her beloved straw cowboy hat over her brows and tightened the chinstrap as she pumped *Banana Pancakes* through the speakers and picked up speed.

Some undressed to their swimsuits. Some held their arms out in front of them and took selfies with their phones along the railing. They seemed like a good enough crowd. A pair of semielderly folks and possibly their grown children and spouses? The woman from a random couple wore a suit right out of a porn film, but that was okay. This was Ibis Island, a place to come and let loose.

Zoe spotted them long before the tour group. A mother and

her calf. And three adults further north. Today would be a good day.

Family. The pod was most likely family. Zoe imagined the mother dolphin as her sister Willow with her six-year-old Chloe and the three others as Seth, Raine, and herself. They'd been that way once, hadn't they? Carefree, playing in and around the island they called home.

She didn't announce the sight of them, and instead let the group discover their presence as she slowed the boat and flanked the female and infant. A few 'Ooos' and 'Awws' alerted the rest of the group to which side of the boat they should watch. "This is a mother and her calf. The infant looks to be about a year old and will stay with the mother for approximately five years." They took pictures and video clips with their phones, watching the water in all the wrong places for an arching body or a fin.

"If you look, you can see spots where the water looks like a large glass plate. The area will be smooth, unlike the choppy water around it. Those are the spots to watch." She would keep them here for about fifteen minutes or until some of the guests lost interest and sat back in their chairs. So, she killed the engine.

Her phone buzzed in her back pocket. Anyone that knew her knew she was out on a tour. She didn't answer.

FIVE

The adult dolphins were active, playful, and jumped completely out of the water. It made Zoe smile as much as the first time she'd seen it. Starting the boat, she inched closer to them, letting the group get a better look.

Her phone buzzed again. It could be Dane. An emergency? He would page her on the walkie. She decided to ignore it again.

After longer than she'd planned, she moved the group along. "Let's head out to the sandbar. On the way we'll get a good look at one of the last fisheries in the Gulf of Mexico, see some of the best places to eat, and check out the bird sanctuary."

Double buzz. The whoever left a message. She could check it when the group took a dip in the water at the sandbar.

Hordes of pelicans and shorebirds hung out on abandoned piers and half-sunken wooden boats. Some flew by close enough that Zoe could hear the rush of the wind beneath its wings. Irritated calls came from the birds that had to move over and give it room on the rotting planks.

As they passed the fishery, Zoe explained that men still went out for two weeks at a time, much like they did decades ago. One of the guys closer to Zoe's age took pictures of the weathered wood and rows of boats. Smart. Most tourists took shots of themselves standing in front of the open water. Not that those shots wouldn't be nice, but the ones that could hang on a wall were the ones of the wildlife, the aging piers, and the half-sunken boats.

She had a photo much like the one he was taking, blown up to wall-hanging size and hung in her home. It was one Seth had given her and was better than any store bought piece of art she'd found.

"The bird sanctuary is off limits to the public. Marine conservationists, permit holders, and biologists only. But that doesn't mean we can't get a closer look." She described the fish hawks that stalked like vultures. The red crested frigate birds as big as eagles that rested in clusters on the branches. "The area beneath us is called The Kitchen. Notice how large and shallow it is? The thick sea grasses carry more than ten kinds of fish all within striking distance for the birds."

Another buzz. This time it was the signal for a text. She was popular today.

She set the anchor and jumped out right into the muck of it. Gathering some of the sea grasses, she dug out a tiny starfish, setting it on the hand of an interested tourist. Digging through the slime, she found another, then another, and finally what she was looking for…a seahorse. "Take as many pictures as you'd like, then return them to the water, please. Thank you."

When she headed out further from Sun Trips pier, she picked a sand bar that wasn't already populated. She killed the engine and dropped the anchor once more. "We'll stay here for about a half hour. This is a good spot for a swim. There are sand dollars in this area. You'll feel them with your feet. Feel free to pick one, but only one, to take with you. You'll also find schools of smaller fish and probably some hermit crabs. And stay toward the front of the boat, please. Feel that current? I don't want to have to chase you down."

Several grabbed snorkels and masks and set out. The elderly mother stayed to watch. She smiled at Zoe and offered an explanation, although it wasn't necessary. "Don't quite have my sea legs anymore."

Gazing at the sand, Zoe imagined Luciana's treasure. An edge of a necklace sticking out of the sand. The rounded edge of a silver plate. A wave of sadness blew over her before she remembered her messages. She pulled out her phone and read the text.

The caller I.D. said St. Petersburg Police Department.

`'zoe. i have something for you at the station. -Matt'`

Finally. It lifted her mood enough that she straightened in her captain's chair. Had she been slouching?

As she thought of the photos on her camera, she kept an eye on the group, making sure they weren't veering off too far. The pictures she'd taken of Detective Osborne's maps would be invaluable to her search. If some murdered dude was still there after who knew how many years, she could certainly justify her search for evidence of what happened to her brother.

A hint of suspicion brushed by her like the wings of one of the swooping pelicans, blowing a few strands of her hair. Connections, possibilities. Like something was trying to get her attention, but she wouldn't let it. Couldn't let it.

"Miss, do you think my son could get an extra sand dollar for me?"

"Hmm?" Zoe turned her head to the woman. She was pretty. Her strong accent said England or Australia. "Of course." Zoe tried for her warmest smile. "If you let it dry out, then run bleach over it, it will turn the brightest color of white."

Dane waited for her tour boat to return. It was another Zoe Clearwater habit he'd picked up recently. Greg and Lilly leaned outside the door of the gift shop, waiting to check in the tourists after they docked. If it were one of them who captained the boat, sure, he'd wait to make sure the customers were happy and his equipment was intact. But with Zoe, he trusted her like he trusted his own hand.

Her signature straw cowboy hat dipped low over her forehead. It was to protect her face and neck from the sun, she always said. He thought it just looked sexy. She wore a bright pink tank that read, 'Sun Trips Touring' in purple block letters across the back. It was one of the older ones, from before she asked him to buy her out.

Customers were happy when they returned from a trip with Zoe. Comfortable, relaxed, satisfied. Her tips were ridiculously large. Yet, she put every penny in the community jar.

The money was good since they merged. He had enough to take a week, maybe a month, out to the spot off the coast of Australia he'd had his eye on. He'd been researching the sweet spot and was sure he could dig up a load. He sighed. The merger also meant nearly double the hours. And with the season picking up? He shook his head as the boat came closer.

Zoe's blonde ponytail brushed her shoulder blades as she moved her head from one side to the other, answering customer's questions, laughing. She had the best laugh, deep and honest. He grimaced. He sure as hell wasn't making any trips until he found the bastard who laid his hands on her.

It had been almost a week, and his adrenaline still spiked when he thought of it just as much as the day he found out. Glancing down at his hands, they were bunched in tight fists. He loosened them as he headed toward his approaching pontoon. In an effort at casual, he greeted her like it was something he did regularly. Since she would know it wasn't, she eyed him with suspicion. He winked. She rolled her eyes. It was their custom.

Grabbing the bow, he released the twined rope and secured it to the pier. She let down the tiny bridge and thanked the tourists for using Sun Trips Touring, reminding them to take their sand dollars. Zoe and her sand dollars. The customers loved that kind of thing. How did she know this shit?

"How was it?" he asked as she straightened the deck and checked corners for anything left behind.

She may not be the stick figure she was in high school, but the muscles in her back and arms still held the definition of an active woman. He kept an eye on her as he helped stack chairs and adjust the blinds for the evening tour. She set her hat on her chair, pulled the band from her hair, and shook her head. Blonde locks dipped over her shoulders in the slightest of waves. The sight wasn't a model posing for a photo shoot. It wasn't a woman trying to attract attention. It was quick and purposeful and took nearly every ounce of sense from his head and sent it south.

She stopped short when she noticed him watching her, noticed him staring. Her eyes darted toward the gift shop. He looked over his shoulder and noticed Lilly elbow Greg in the ribs and stifle a laugh with the back of her hand.

"Just loosening the dandruff," she snarled.

"They were a quiet group. Nice people," she added.

She bent over to get her bag, her hair falling around one of her tanned shoulders. A familiar scent of fresh salt water and honeysuckle blew into his lungs. She straightened and took a step toward the boat's mini pier. Those perky B cups—possibly C cups—nearly ran right into him.

Backing up, she sighed. "I need to make a run to St. Pete's and get back in time for the party cruise. Is there something I can do for you?"

He wiggled his brows up and down once.

"Nice try, Romeo." She huffed and skirted around him.

The blood must be coming back to his head, because he remembered. "Liam is on for the party cruise tonight."

"I'm taking his shift. He covered for me last weekend when you went behind my back and convinced my parents I could have a deathly case of the bends."

Liam wasn't the one who covered for her. "I told you we used your sick days."

She stopped her feet and twisted her head, looking as guilty as a kid who just hocked a candy bar from a corner drug store. "Keep your voice down. You helped me out with my boat. Thanks, okay? But we've already been seen together. It's hard enough to fit in around here."

"St. Pete's?" he asked ignoring her tirade. "You're going to see the cop?"

She walked around the back side of the gift shop to the break room door. His interest in her trip to St. Petersburg almost took his mind off the mention of the attack at her parents' house.

"I think my camera is ready," she said and slowed down, letting him catch up.

"I'm coming with you." He opened the door for her and stepped back.

She did that twisting her head thing again.

"That's right, Zoe," he said sarcastically. "We wouldn't want to be caught, two people who work here, alone in the common break room."

Quick as hell, she elbowed him as she passed. How did he not see that coming?

"You can come, but I'm not driving out of the parking lot with you again."

"You can't be serious."

She gave him her look that said she could be.

"Ya know." He stepped closer, making her back up against a

43

wall. "If people are talking, we could give them something to talk about." He meant it as a joke, but the scent of her filled his head and fogged his mind. He knew his eyes had dropped to her lips, but he couldn't seem to get them to move.

The slightest tremble ran through her defined shoulders before she pushed him away with both hands. "It's not funny. You don't hear them."

His employees? They did that? "Okay. I'll meet you at your parents' restaurant, buy you a bite to eat, then we can leave from there together."

"I don't have time to eat, but I'll meet you there. I want to say 'hey' to the shrimp. Chloe's been hanging at the restaurant since she's out of school for the summer."

He knew this, of course. Willow's daughter was a younger version of her mom. Long blonde hair, knobby knees. The cutest kindergarten graduate there was. "It's a date."

"If you call it a date, you're not coming."

He tried to listen, really he did. But a stray lock of her silky hair eluded the rest and covered her shoulder. Using the tips of his fingers, he ran them from her collarbone and over the shoulder that was just as silky as the hair. It was the third time since she'd docked that he noticed her shiver in the warm Florida air.

———

Zoe made sure she drove this time. She needed to stay in control. They rode in her Jeep—her practical Jeep. She'd left the top down letting the Gulf breeze whip her ponytail and fill her senses. It was more soothing than any of the incense or chamomile tea her mother gave her. Gripping the steering wheel, she turned up her playlist. *Little Pink Houses*. *I'm Yours*. Easy, comfortable.

Dane hadn't spoken much on their forty-five minute drive to St. Petersburg. His sandy brown hair flipped around his face as he looked out the passenger side of the jeep on 275 north.

Her reaction to his proximity on the boat had been humiliating. And the break room? She could kick herself. He had been close, that was all. She'd been on her male moratorium for how long now? Since Seth's disappearance? Ouch. That was a secret no one needed to know about.

He was Dane Corbin. He used his looks to play the part of scuba diving expert and successful owner of the playful yet reliable Sun Trips Touring. His reputation as man slut and treasure hunter didn't hurt business, that she was sure of. He used it all in his favor. She could hardly blame him. That didn't mean she had to add herself to the list of girls who reacted to his proximity.

"Are you going to exit?" he raised his voice over the wind.

Oh shit. She checked her mirror and swerved. "Sorry about that. I was thinking about work tonight," she lied. "Do you know how many we have signed up? I did both the morning and afternoon snorkeling/eco tours and didn't get a chance to look."

"Five men, three women. All twenty-somethings." Then, he dropped his voice to almost a whisper. "Just make sure you don't anchor."

She knew this, of course. Sun Trips Touring let customers drink alcohol on their evening party boats, but no swimming.

Pulling into the closest spot in the St. Petersburg Police Department lot, she set her mind to the pictures on her camera. She would have just enough time between cruises to take the photos from the detective's map and add the information to her own.

She grabbed her purse, then dropped her keys in the opening and slid down, skipping the running board and landing soundly on her feet. The bends, her ass.

"Come on, boss. I want to take a look at the pictures on my

camera before work tonight. Do you think they left the one of the skull?" A fast wave of needles skittered from the top of her head to the bottom of her feet.

He shrugged and set his hand comfortably on the back of her elbow. They weren't standing in front of Sun Trips. It wasn't like he was trying to hold her hand or slide an arm around her, or worse yet, place his hand on her back. It was a sign of support, so she ignored her deprived hormones and accepted the platonic gesture as they entered the police department.

Stopping at reception, Zoe told the young man that Detective Osborne was expecting her. They sat in the nearest chairs. Dane shook his knee as they waited silently. What did he have to be nervous about?

The detective came out of the elevators looking expectantly in her direction. He paused when his eyes turned to Dane but not for long. In his hand, he held a thick manila envelope. Unfortunately, her camera was puny enough to actually fit into an envelope. She rocked on the balls of her feet, anxious to get to the pictures she took of his maps.

He extended his hand before fully reaching the two of them.

Dane took a small step in front of her and grabbed it. "Detective," he nodded as he shook.

"Mr. Corbin," Detective Osborne answered flatly. "Zoe's boss," he added.

She was thankful Dane stepped in to help the last time they were here. She would admit to being a bit overwhelmed, but this was rude. Elbowing him in the arm, she stepped around him. "Thank you for the messages, Detective. You have my camera?"

The detective ran a hand over his deep brown hair as he held out the envelope. A few strands of gray caught the florescent lights. She took the envelope as Dane crowded her again. What the hell? She set her elbow on his ribs this time, then pushed.

"I'm afraid the camera stays in evidence until the investigation is complete," the detective said as he stood tall and his gaze moved between her and Dane.

This time she nearly tripped as Dane stepped in front of her. "You called us all the way out here to pick up Zoe's camera." She didn't like the way he used the word, 'us.'

"Actually," she admitted. "The message said he had something for me. I guess I assumed."

So, what was in the envelope? Should she just rip it open right here?

It appeared the detective didn't appreciate Dane's assertive posture, because he reached in front of Dane and took the back of Zoe's arm. Pulling her away a few feet, he said in a low voice, "Go ahead and open it. I can't give you the camera since it is evidence in an open investigation, but I developed the photos for you."

She froze for a moment, taking in the idea of doing without her camera for…how long? Realizing he must have done her some kind of a favor, she shook her head once and said, "You did that for me," then ripped open the top of the envelope. "Thank you." Now that she thought of it, the envelope was too heavy for just her underwater camera. Seth may not have approved of her dinky camera, but she'd spent a hunk of her salary on it. Looking closer, she reached in and fanned through the pictures. "You printed *all* of my pictures?" She jerked her gaze upward. He was very tall and his proximity disconcerting, but the light brown in his eyes was warm and reminded her of the sand.

He partially glanced in Dane's direction making her check on him, too. His eyes were most definitely not warm as he stood with his chest out and elbows locked at his sides. Testosterone could be so annoying.

The detective turned fully away from Dane this time. "You didn't listen to the voice mail I left you, did you?"

"Honestly, I was so excited about my camera I forgot all about it."

"Of course. I'm sorry about that. It's procedure. I tell you what. You keep the photos. Listen to your voice mail when you get a chance." He moved his gaze over his shoulder, "And call me if you'd like to."

"If I'd like to," she repeated flatly. She didn't really catch onto his cryptic message and truly just wanted to dig into the photos. "I'll do that. Thank you…" She still didn't have her camera. "…I think."

Dane took a step closer, his hard shoulder pressed against hers. "If that's all you've got for us, we'll be going then." Sarcasm dripped from his tone.

Her mind wasn't on Dane's sarcasm and only partially on the detective's allusiveness. It was on the pictures. Would he have developed the one of the skull? What kind of detail could she get from the maps if she blew up a print?

Dane placed his hand on her back as he opened the door for her but she only partially noticed. As she thumbed through the photos, she swiped her phone and held it between her check and shoulder.

She chose voice mail. "This is Detective Osborne. I left you a text message and realized that was lame."

'Lame?'

"The truth is I developed the photos from your camera. I'm hoping it will sway you to have dinner with me." At the end, he added quickly, "Unless you and Mr. Corbin are an item."

'Sway me? An item?' He sounded a bit like her father. It was cute.

He left his personal number before he disconnected. Detective Osborne. She strolled toward the door blindly. Tall. Attractive. Hair cut tightly that was nearly the color of hers. He must be nearly her brother's age. Or the age he was when he disappeared—died.

She didn't realize Dane was waiting for her by the driver's side of her jeep. "Was that about the camera?"

She jerked. "Was what about the camera?" Oh, the voice mail. "No." Oh jeez, she was blushing. She could feel it. Not now. Not now in front of Dane. "It was nothing."

SIX

Dane couldn't remember a single time Zoe had trouble with a tour group. She held her own, and he always booked party boats well under regulation capacity, especially when only one captain was scheduled. So, why was he sitting on the picnic table in the outdoor waiting area at ten o'clock on a Friday night instead of kicking up his heels at Show Me's?

Because her tour group had shown up in a cab. And that could be a good sign or a bad sign. A good sign that the party boat customers weren't planning on drinking and driving and a bad sign that they planned on getting loaded enough to need a cab. He reminded himself—again—there was only so much they could drink on a ninety-minute ride with no bathroom.

The lights from the distant bridge turned the water into rippling black glass. He stood each time a boat trolled, its headlight bright enough to seem like a portable lighthouse.

Zoe had built the waiting area with her own hands. A roof, three benches, and a picnic table. He sat on top of the table with his walkie on his thigh, watching the edge of the water. It was his idea to paint everything blue. It was her mother's idea to cover it with sea turtles and shore birds. Harmony had also added the sign that read, 'No Shoes, No Shirt, No Problem.' What a woman.

The beach was shut down for the night. No lights were allowed anywhere on land along the waterfront during turtle nesting season. He thought of the female loggerheads that might be crawling up the sand at that moment. The ten miles of beach on the west side of Ibis alone brought nearly two hundred nests last year. Zoe said they were on track for that many again.

The dunes to the south of Sun Trips were a preferred nesting spot. What did Richard Beckett have in mind for the property? He doubted it was a turtle-friendly plan. The next lazy bob of light aimed straight for his docking pier. He stood, then sat again.

She wouldn't want anyone to see him wait for her twice in one day. But, he was the boss, dammit. And they were the only two left. He tossed his walkie on the table and made his way to the pier.

No music came through the speakers of the boat. His face fell as he noted the quiet was all wrong. Carefully, she flanked the pier. The riders sat with their hands in their laps. One looked like booze and boating hadn't mixed well with his stomach.

"Welcome back, ladies and gentlemen," Zoe announced. "I hope you enjoyed your ride. We have bathrooms just inside the doors and to the right. I see your cab making the turn off Pelican Bridge right now."

She was soaking wet. One of the girls snickered as she gave her a look, then snorted. Another one of the girls joined in as they exited the boat one at a time. The dude in the middle walked with his knees together, his nuts in his hands…and also wet. The scenario was coming together.

Dane gave Zoe a once over. She looked like she was in one piece. He tied the boat as if it was something he always did, then helped check the gear and straighten the chairs. "Thank you for coming," he said as they exited one by one. He wasn't sure if he should invite them to come back again or not.

Beer cans were recycled, garbage tossed, and the boat readied for the first snorkeling/eco tour scheduled for the morning. Without pausing, Dane asked, "Drunk fell overboard?"

Zoe slung her tiny purse over her shoulder. "Yep."

He adjusted a buoy that was knotted and hadn't fallen completely between the boat and the pier. "You had to go in after him?"

"Right again." They headed for the office to check the group back in.

"That doesn't explain why he was holding his jewels like they were jewels."

"He fell overboard on purpose to get me in the water with him."

Dane's first reaction was a deep desire to follow the dude into the bathroom and teach the little prick what happens when you take advantage of…of what? His girl? She wasn't. She'd made that clear at St. Pete's police station when they met the detective. Was she just a friend who grew up on the same island as he did? Shit.

Then, he smiled. Smiled from ear to ear. "And you gave his junk a hearty slam with what…your knee I assume?"

"You assume right."

His brows dropped. It wasn't the first time in the past week she had a man come at her physically. "I'm following you home."

After all he just said, *this* was the comment that made her stop and face him?

She tilted her head, looked him in the eyes and took a deep breath. "I'll be in at eight to ready the pontoon for the snorkel tour." She walked into the office area, stood behind the check-in desk and artificially smiled at the first girl in the line.

Zoe dried her hair from her shower just enough to pass as presentable, slapped on some makeup, and waited in her front room for Raine to get there. She didn't own Sun Trips anymore and couldn't ban that drunk jerk from ever returning. She had to just take it. Well, take it after she swatted his wandering hands and kneed him soundly in the nuts. Guys and their nuts. A few drinks with her sisters and she'd be good as new. Although Detective Osborne didn't develop the photo of the knife through the skull, she still needed to fill them in on her visit to St. Pete's. And her possible dinner date.

She loved her little two-bedroom house. She'd earned it. The money made from her business—her old business—all went either into reinvesting in Sun Trips Touring or into this house. The money Dane paid for her half would cover the house payments and bills for at least a few more years. For now, she was smart and pinching her budget wherever she could.

She'd turned away from the style of the eccentric island home she grew up in. Hers was simple, uncluttered and…her. The soft yellow walls of the living room spoke to her, subtle yet inviting. A simple slate blue couch and love seat with floor lamp between. A wicker coffee table and small flat-screen TV for the moments she never watched television. When was the last time she turned the thing on? Her phone buzzed. It was Willow? She jogged out the front door, locking it behind her.

"Willow," Zoe said, surprised to see her in the passenger seat of Raine's pickup. "How did you get away?"

"Mom and Dad are keeping Chloe. The bar is fully staffed. I heard about your tour group."

"You heard about my night? It just happened."

Dane. Sometimes he and Willow were closer friends than Zoe liked.

More important than her tour group, Zoe asked, "Aren't you afraid, you know, about letting Chloe stay with them? At that house?" She didn't mean it exactly the way it came out. But whoever broke in was still out there.

"They came over to my place for euchre. Chloe won. They offered to stay after Dane called."

No snide remark from Raine about the reference to Dane. That probably wasn't a good sign. It didn't go unnoticed. "Is Show Me's okay?" Raine asked.

Shrugging, Zoe answered. "I'm getting drunk. Where is not a factor."

Raine huffed. "Your getting drunk is two full-leaded beers instead of light ones."

They pulled up to the bar. An ostentatiously jacked turquoise blue Jeep sat in the asphalt parking lot. "Did you tell Dane where we were going?"

Willow answered as she slid out of the truck. "I may have mentioned it as a possibility, but nothing for certain. Not that there are a lot of choices on the island. I need a break from Luciana's."

"But I haven't been to your bar in—"

"That's silly," Willow opened Zoe's door, took her arm, and wrapped it firmly in hers. "We probably won't even see Dane."

That would be impossible. If Dane Corbin was here, everyone would know it. Show Me's was booming, literally and metaphorically. She could feel the beat of the music out here. The owner had added a gift shop to the lobby, redecorated the dance floor, and expanded further onto the beach. He bought up some random lots to add parking spots for the complimentary valet parking Raine refused to use.

The place was too formal for an island. Island bars should have walls open to the outside, vivid colors and character. Show Me's may have decent food and plenty of company, but the atmosphere was boring. Zoe greeted the bouncer as they passed. "Hello, Eli. We won't be any trouble tonight," she told him sarcastically.

"The three Clearwater sisters? I'm calling for backup. How's the shelter doing?"

Eli could build anything, even a shelter on a roof for a handful of goats. "Sturdy as ever. You're a genius."

"Damnedest thing I've ever made," he said as they passed him and looked around for a table.

The air was thick. Between the humidity of June and jiggling bodies on the dance floor, Zoe was thankful the owner added a beer garden.

"I'm going to check on the lighting outside," Raine yelled over the sound of thumping. She had a one-track mind. "I'll be right back."

"What are you going to do if it isn't turtle friendly? Hunt up Blake Eaton at this hour?" Zoe asked.

Raine had an evil grin she saved for anything involving a good fight for the turtles. It was just in the last few years they were making a statistical comeback, as small as it was. There was no stopping Raine now.

"It wouldn't be a first offense," Raine reminded her.

Slinging the long strap of her tiny purse over her shoulder, Zoe maneuvered around a few side tables, heading for an empty one she spotted in a corner.

"Don't look now," Willow said.

As if that comment ever made anyone do anything other than look. Dane Corbin could find treasure in spots no one else did, he could run a business with his eyes closed, and he was a hell of a good dancer. The ladies ate it up, locals and tourists alike. Zoe did a one-eighty and headed for the bar. Willow didn't question and followed.

"MGD. Bottle," she said to the bartender before turning to Willow. "What do you want to drink?"

"Amaretto Stone Sour," Willow answered.

The bartender looked to Zoe. "Lite?"

Zoe squinted. "Leaded."

The bartender turned to take care of their order as Zoe leaned against the bar. She didn't want to face the dance floor. "Amaretto Stone Sour? You've been drinking that since high school."

"Slurping beer from a bottle isn't much to brag about." Willow made her way around Zoe, making her rotate to face the dance floor again. Dane had two girls twerking their butts at him. He turned his eyes to Zoe and kept them there. She could see the cobalt color all the way from the dance floor to where she stood at the bar. Goosebumps erupted on her arms and a chill scurried up her back and over her scalp.

"MGD?" Willow. "After your second one of those, I might have to carry you home."

"Let's sit." Zoe pulled Willow away as she took a long drink. The table in the corner was still empty.

From behind, an arm slid around the front of her. It wasn't like the intruder had done. And it obviously wasn't the arm of the man who attacked her, but she flinched anyway.

"Dance with me," a breathy voice whispered in her ear.

Zoe grabbed the arm with both hands and reactively pushed it away so she could get a look. Thick leather bracelet. Raised veins over strands of muscle. It was him. She turned and faced a thinner band of leather around his neck, then lifted her gaze to the sandy brown hair that threatened to cover the blue in his eyes. The strength of his body mixed with the close proximity and unnerved her to the point of making her shiver.

From the time she was a child, her parents taught the four of them to dance around the makeshift fire pit in their backyard.

She could waltz, tango, and even do the two-step. She could jiggle by herself, dancing praises for their fortune as she pranced around the fire. She could most definitely *not* do what was happening out on Show Me's dance floor.

"This isn't high school, Dane," Raine interrupted as she joined them. "She's not going to fall for you ever again."

"How many years are you gonna hold on to that one?" Dane may bite his tongue when he was with their parents, but not so much when they weren't around.

"Not that I don't appreciate you sticking up for me, big sister, but that was cold, even for you."

The creases between Raine's eyes relaxed. "You're right. I'm sorry, Dane. Not in such a great mood. I just found uncovered lights in plain sight of two turtle nests. Blake Eaton had better be glad it's too early for either of them to hatch, or I'd march over and bang on his doors right now."

"Call a truce and dance with him, Zoe. We'll find a table." Willow took the beer from Zoe's hand and pulled Raine along.

Well, it wasn't like that made a diff—

In a highly public gesture, Dane linked fingers with her and led the way. The music wasn't slow, but it wasn't fast either...so that was something. Bongo drums thumped and something with a twang rang in the background. She couldn't back down from Dane Corbin with nearly every pair of female eyes trained on her. He stopped center stage, of course.

Turning to face her, he grasped her hips. He smirked as he stood without moving, then lifted a corner of his mouth. At just over six foot, he stood a full half-foot taller than her. She wasn't wearing heels tonight.

Playboy jerk.

In return, she slapped her hands on his shoulders. She should have chosen his wrists or maybe his elbows because his shoulders were lean, warm, and flexed under her grip. The squint she volleyed back at him must have hit its target, because he clasped his fingers tighter on her hips, jerking them to his. Defying her will, waves of heat spread from her core outward to every inch of her body.

And then he started moving. Strong hands pushed and pulled, guiding her hips with the pounding of the beat. They moved in their circle, forward and back, rotating clockwise, reversing left then right. No wonder the girls wanted to dance with him. She didn't have a chance to make a fool of herself. Although torture couldn't have made her admit it, she was having fun. She didn't need to watch her feet or the floor. Though she told herself repeatedly it wasn't sensual, it was exactly that.

No more than an inch separated their fluid movements. As if trusting her, he let go of one of her hips, sliding his hand up her waist. His thumb brushed the side of her breast before trailing around to the middle of her back. Another wave of heat shivered through her.

He slipped a thigh between hers, scissoring her legs when they moved to the side. His hard thighs guided hers. They were warm and she had to concentrate to keep her eyes from rolling to the back of her head. Her breasts moved against his chest as their bodies rotated. His hip pressed into hers when he wanted her to step back. Like a magnet needing its positive charge, she followed when that hip turned away.

His cheeks were flushed, the veins over his temples pulsed. His jaws flex as the waves of heat seared back through her arms and legs and landed like a tsunami in her center. She convinced herself the sweat that formed at the base of her neck was from the movements and dozens of bodies clustered around them. Not from the dancing.

They'd known each other long enough to interpret gestures and read the meaning behind their stares. Had they broken eye contact since the song started? The cobalt blue was deep and bold, like the entrance to the hidden cavern Zoe found.

The image of the skull blew past her vision, bringing her out of her sensual trance. Good thing since the next song was slow, and she had lost all trust in her body's reactions to deal with something slow. She could not fall for Dane Corbin. Not now. Not ever.

SEVEN

They hadn't spoken during their dance, not out loud anyway. It was appreciated since that meant Zoe didn't get caught yelling at the top of her lungs when the song stopped. As she pulled away from the dance floor, he grabbed her hand and stopped her. She had to use so much force to make her getaway, they might have tumbled to the ground in opposite directions if he let go.

He gave in and let her lead them toward the bar, but he clasped her hand tight enough she couldn't let go. She recited small chants in her head, reminding herself he would have been dancing that same dance with some other girl if Zoe hadn't showed. Somehow the fact that he chose her instead of one of the others wasn't getting the right response from her libido.

"Second round, please," Zoe practically yelled. It was time to make sure Dane knew where they stood. Where did they stand again?

Oh, right. Boss. Not boss.

Playboy. Girl who doesn't want a playboy.

World traveler. Small island girl.

"You're thinking." He stood much too close for her chanting to do any damned good.

She took her beer. "Some women do that. You probably don't know any."

Dane handed the bartender some money before Zoe could get to it.

She took a deep drink. It was cold and crisp. She felt it in her thighs.

"You didn't ask me what I wanted to drink," he said low in her ear. He stepped away, making her want to pull him back. He brushed her nose with his thumb and said, "You have something there."

She knew what it was. She burned it in the sun. It was slight, but enough to peel.

"Is that what girls do for you? Get your drinks? Because I'm not one of them. And I have a fungus on my nose. You'd better go wash your hands."

His smile was beautiful, warm, and familiar. And it was cheating. She sighed, suddenly defeated. Closing her eyes tighter than she wanted, she dipped her head. "I'm going to find my sisters, Dane. Consider the truce paid in full." She turned away from him but then thought differently. Spinning on her heels before he could get away, she added, "And thank you," but he was there, close enough to feel the rise and fall of his chest against hers.

His eyes dropped to her mouth as he dipped his head closer. With both hands, she pushed him away as her heartbeat shot up and her chest heaved. "See you tomorrow." Her heart told her to turn around, but thankfully her head made her feet walk away.

Her sisters sat at a tiny table in the center of the tightly-fit section. They both had their brows lifted high.

Willow smirked. Raine crossed her arms. Zoe took two long swigs before sitting down with them.

"Need a cigarette?" Raine asked.

Zoe waved her hand like she was shooing a fly. "Don't be silly." She took another, longer swig, emptying her bottle completely. It might cool the embarrassment that crept up her neck and surely filled her cheeks.

Willow smiled.

"What?" This was not happening.

"You danced." Willow said flatly in direct contrast to the smirk on her face. "With Dane Corbin. It was hot. I've never seen him do that before."

"Now, you're just being stupid." Zoe knew this, at least, was true. "He dances like that with anything with breasts. Raine? Help me out, here."

Raine shook her head. "I have to agree with Willow on this one and not just because I feel guilty for the way I treated him earlier, although I do."

"I'm sure he's doing the same thing with some other—"

"He left after you didn't let him kiss you by the bar," Raine said.

"Alone," Willow added.

Zoe worked hard to avoid Dane. It wasn't healthy to obsess about something that wasn't meant to be. And avoiding was working well. Ultimate Frisbee on Sundays. Walking her section of the beach on her assigned days each week. She found and staked an average of three nests per morning. Raine was right. Nesting season would be big again this year. Captaining the tour boats kept her away from the shop and from him.

The occasional text messages from the detective helped. He was sweet. They planned on getting together Friday night for dinner. His texts sometimes reminded Zoe of her parents. She realized her parents were a young middle-fifties, but the similarities were still disconcerting. Disconcerting, but cute.

Today was for show. Zoe couldn't avoid the gift shop forever. She needed to prove to the other employees she wasn't sleeping with the boss. It was the only theory the guys had come up with as to why Dane would have bought a business that kept him from his frequent treasure hunting trips. If she were honest with herself, she wasn't even sure why he agreed to her request.

She shouldn't get to skip gift shop duty, and she did trash duty like everyone else. She checked off customers for boat tours and signed them in when they returned. In between, she answered questions, ran the register, and straightened up racks of clothes. She—actually Dane—got in a new shipment of sandals, some for men and some for women. As dumb as it was, it felt a little like Christmas.

Fair enough, she decided, as she organized the display. She was the one who insisted on selling versus a true merger. She'd spent that past several months walking the line between convincing her former employees they had to answer to Dane—because she was no longer their boss—and still using her skills as lead boat captain.

A man of at least fifty came in. He was alone and dressed in weathered shorts, leather sandals, and a faded button-down shirt. His hair was long and braided. Small hoop earrings hung in each lobe and tattoos covered his right forearm and left calf. The size of the rings on his fingers and the pendant hanging from his neck rounded the package and screamed, 'treasure hunter.' A good-looking man, definitely, but not her type. And what was it with her sudden interest in older men? Salt and pepper hair curled just over his ears. He was well over six foot, blue eyes. Not the solid blue of Dane's, more of a crystal blue, like a husky's. It must be her sex moratorium.

"Can I help you with anything?" She smiled. He smiled back. Whoops. Gold tooth. Definitely not her type.

"This Dane Corbin's place?" He held out his hand, and she took it.

They shook as she answered. "It is now, yes. He's running some errands. Can I leave him a message?"

The man turned his gaze downward. "No. I'll catch up with him soon enough." His eyes ran over her shop—Dane's shop. It made her uncomfortable. She'd built it, decorated it, stocked it, and restocked it. It might not be hers, but she still took pride in it.

"This doesn't look like Dane."

"Oh? How do you know each other, if you don't mind me asking?"

"Nah. Name's Nemo. Lucky Nemo. Named before the movie." He winked.

Yes, cute but not her style.

Thumbing through some of the key chains on display, he spoke like he was reminiscing. "Dane and I have spent days, sometimes weeks together."

Treasure hunter. She was right.

"He's been hanging low lately." Lucky turned in a circle and squinted. "And for this, I guess."

She didn't like his tone. Zoe leaned her hip on the back of the chair customers used to try on shoes. "His business doubled recently," she said defensively. Did several months count as recently? "We're old high school friends." Why did she add that? She shrugged. "He's been busy. What's it like out there in the middle of the ocean?"

He turned to face her and tilted his head. "You haven't had this conversation with him, old *friend*?"

She was caught off guard. She hadn't, actually. He never discussed his treasure hunting, and she never asked. Now, she felt like a heel. "He doesn't talk about it."

"You're serious." Another statement.

"Is that strange?"

"Strange? Dane doesn't miss many chances to tell about his best haul or the next place he wants to hit."

He said it like they were planning bank robberies.

A customer brought a shark tooth necklace and a pair of trunks to the sales counter. She hoped Lucky wouldn't leave. He walked around like a tourist, except he shook his head back and forth every now and then.

"Thank you for coming," she told the boy with the shark tooth. "Have a nice day." She turned her head away from Lucky but kept her eyes on him.

"Did he tell you about the deep sea dive off the west coast of the Hawaiian islands?" he asked her.

She shook her head. It felt like an apology.

"Mostly silver place settings. The price of silver is up these days." He smiled wide making his gold tooth glint in the florescent lights. "How about the Smithsonian? Of course he told you about the Smithsonian."

"The Smithsonian? You mean as in *thee* Smithsonian? Dane donated something to a museum? I thought he sold everything he found." The last part came out wrong. Or it came out right but shouldn't have come out at all.

"Calypso's ship. Divers thought they'd cleaned it, but Dane has a knack at finding hidden compartments." Lucky brushed his wavy hair over an ear and leaned in. He looked like he could be a model for a rock star magazine. "He could have bought this island for what he gave up." He shook his head in obvious disgust.

"Are you telling me Dane Corbin donated millions of dollars' worth of treasure?"

"Not millions, sweetheart, but he probably doesn't want me to say. Not if he hasn't offered up the information himself. And not some of the pieces. It brings tears to my eyes, but he gave up the entire haul. I'm sure it brought real tears to the geeks at the Institute."

She wanted to listen to him longer. Ask him more questions that hadn't come to her yet. Her elbows found their way to the glass counter near the cash register. She rested her chin in her hands as he spoke of the dangers they'd encountered. Sharks and competing divers. The times they searched for weeks and came up empty handed.

Apparently, Lucky was the wheels—or boat owner—and Dane was the one with the intuition. The bell rang on the front door. She barely heard it and didn't offer a greeting. It was Dane.

He hardly ever walked through the front. He stopped short when he saw Lucky and frowned. "Lucky Nemo," he said cautiously. "What brings you to the island?"

Tomorrow was a beach walk day. It took Zoe days to recover from her near-kiss with Dane and a few more to wrap her head around his donation to the Smithsonian. Beach walking served as therapy.

She crawled into bed and thumbed through her phone before turning out the lights. There was something about crawling into a crisply made bed. It was more soothing than her mother's raspberry tea.

She'd gotten into the habit of texting her mother each night, reminding her to lock her doors and windows. Zoe was mostly sure her parents started locking their doors at night—something they'd never done in the thirty-plus years they lived there—but the windows? They preferred to keep their windows open day and night. The mature pines and palm trees that surrounded their house served as reasonable shade from the brutal Florida summer sun. At least her parents thought so.

As a daughter of Henry and Harmony Clearwater, Zoe needed to justify using her air conditioner by turning it up a few degrees. Just as she typed her nightly nag to her mother, her phone buzzed.

'no need to text me, dear. we're locked up nice and safe. love you.'

She was parenting her parents. It had to be done.

'love you too, mom. night.'

As usual, the topic of conversation made her think of their intruder. The feel of his hand on her face, his arm clamped around her neck. It was as fresh as if it happened yesterday. Damn it. Now, she needed to check her locks. Flipping the covers back on her bed, she tossed her legs over the side as her phone buzzed again.

'night? are you going to bed already?'

Zoe walked around her small ranch house, checking locks in the dark as they texted back and forth.

'beach walking tomorrow.'

'still'

'not in high school anymore. I need my sleep.'

'are you pent up, dear? it's not good to let the cobwebs grow in the nether regions.'

Good grief. It was fun to have granola parents except for the times her mother wanted to give her advice on her sex life.

'i like to think of it as purposely independent'

Her phone buzzed twice this time.

'i'm on the island'

'do you need me to bring over new batteries?'

'mom!'

Zoe stood at her living room window laughing out loud.

'i'm not your mom, but i am on the island. you up for a visitor?'

The window. The window was unlocked. She had the air on for three days straight. Her body trembled and froze all at the same time. The lights. Holy shit, she left herself in the dark again.

EIGHT

Grabbing her keys from the hook by the front door, she flew out. She imagined the man chasing her from behind and covered her head with her arms as she ran to her Jeep. It was dark. Her tall trees blocked the streetlights. The gravel under her slippers crunched as she ran, giving away her location to anyone hiding behind the trees. She didn't have the nerve to look.

Except the back seat of the Jeep. She had to check the back of the Jeep. Her hands shook so hard she dropped her phone. Scrambling to pick it up, she plopped in the driver's side and started the engine. She didn't want to look around, but backing up made it necessary.

A man. A man stood at the end of her driveway. She screamed.

"Whoa," he said, holding his hands out at her.

She recognized the voice, but then, no. As she darted her eyes around her, he started waving his arms like he was flagging her down. And he wasn't a small someone. He was tall and wore a gun holster.

"Zoe? It's me, Matt. It's Detective Osborne. You okay? I'm going to walk forward, now. Very slow. Take it easy."

Matt. It was Matt. She pulled the emergency brake, then ran out of her Jeep toward him.

"It's okay. Here, here."

She started laughing. It was sort of a hysterical laugh, but she was laughing. "That's something my father says to me when I'm hysterical."

"Father? Ouch."

She laughed again and looked up at him.

"Do you get hysterical often?" His face was hard to make out. The street light two doors down was visible from this part of the driveway, but it created a halo around his head, darkening his features.

Oh shit. Shit, shit. She must seem like a crazy woman. "My window. It was unlocked." Not helping. "I locked it. I know I did." Did she? "I'm almost positive I did. I've had the air conditioning on for three days straight, and I always, always lock my windows when I shut them." Her shoulders fell. She had a nice man who was actually interested in her—before now—standing in her driveway, and here she stood, acting like a lunatic.

"I heard about the break-in at your parents' home. You have every right to be jittery. Would you like me to take a look around?"

Afraid to open her mouth for fear more words might come out, she nodded and tried to smile. Her arms and legs were like wet noodles, but she made them move as if she were a sane person.

They searched the house, turning on every light. He checked in each closet, under her bed, and behind her couch and loveseat. She stayed on his heels but stopped herself from hanging onto his holster.

"There's no one in here. Do you notice anything out of place?"

She'd been too scared to pay attention. She hadn't noticed anything when she came home, made dinner, or grabbed her shower. "I don't think so."

"Have you taken a good look?"

She shook her head and started strolling through her small home. She was tidy, so that made it easy. It was another one of those things she needed to change from her childhood. No large murals on the siding of her home and no clutter. It fit her parents but not her.

The living room was intact, right down to where she'd left her remote. The kitchen was good, the kitchen nook. Her bedroom was all in place, even the decorative pillows she left on the side of the bed that was never used. Ever.

The extra bedroom was an office. She often brought work home. When she had a business to bring work home from. The top, right desk drawer was open. Only a half-inch or so. She could have done that if a paper had wedged itself between the drawer and top. She reached down to pull it open and realized her laptop was closed. She never closed her laptop.

As if she burned her hand, she pulled it back. Her head turned to Matt, then back again. "I don't leave drawers stuck open, not even partially, and I never, ever close my laptop."

"Don't touch anything, Zoe."

She covered her mouth with both hands as she eyed the room. "I'm acting like a fool," she said between her fingers. "No one's in here." She said the last part for herself.

"Not a fool. Smart. You've been through an attack. Caught an intruder in the act. Caught him in the safety of the place you grew up in."

Wow. He had heard about the break-in.

"It's a feeling of violation and invasion. It takes time to get over something like that."

It made her smile.

"How did you get that scar?" he asked, lifting his arm to her forearm as if he might touch it, then dropping his hand.

She looked up at him again. This close, she noticed his hair truly was the color of hers, minus the gray, of course. "I was doing some pontoon repairs, turned and smacked the corner of the storage compartment with my arm. You sound like my father again."

He let out a sigh and lowered his brows. "That's a problem since I plan on kissing you tomorrow after dinner." His gaze dropped to her mouth.

Dane liked to gaze at her mouth. Bad thought. Bad thought.

"Or maybe before dinner," he added without taking his eyes from her lips.

When she pulled away he looked like he was analyzing her as if she was a crime scene. She smiled, and that seemed to reassure him.

"I should call Chief Roberts."

She nodded, although she thought calling the Ibis Island Chief of Police was useless.

"But keep looking around, will you?" he asked, then took out a pair of plastic gloves from a compartment on his belt. "Here. Wear these and look through your drawers. Check to see if anything is missing, but try not to disturb anything."

Dane convinced himself driving by Zoe's for the third time this week wasn't stalking her, and it couldn't be classified under Peeping Tom. She lived alone, was female, and was attacked a few short weeks ago. He could check on the house as he drove. It was a public street.

Borderline pathetic, was what it was.

Turning the corner, he let the humid evening air blow from the open sides of his Jeep. He dodged a few potholes before slowing down.

The dance. Damned woman. It had him messed up in the head. When had she turned into such a damned sexy woman? Damned sexy, smart, screwed-up woman?

There was a car. There was a black car parked in the street in front of her house. That was a first, and like hell if he wouldn't check on her, now. Tomorrow was one of her days to walk the beach. She should be in bed soon, and yet her lights were on. All of them.

The front door was cracked open. Her windows were closed. Walking up to her house, he heard a man's voice. It didn't sound agitated, but he wasn't taking any chances. Slowly pushing the door, he stepped softly into her living room.

His shoulders relaxed when he heard her voice. And it wasn't hysterical. Except now he was standing in her living room, uninvited, and unannounced when she had a guy over.

She had a guy over?

Before he had a chance to retreat, Matt Osborne came from a back room. "I thought I heard something. It's Dane. Dane Corbin, right?"

"The door was open," Dane explained weakly. "What are you doing here, Detective? I mean, is everything okay? Is it something about the skull?"

"No, the skull case is coming along," he answered as Zoe followed him into the living room.

Dane suddenly had a bad feeling about other reasons the detective might be in Zoe's house at this hour.

Osborne kept on. "Forensics is nearly finished with it. We're hoping to go public with their findings early next week. Excuse me for being forward, but since I have a date with Zoe tomorrow night and you've walked into her house at this hour without knocking, I feel like I should ask…is there something…" He waved his hand between Zoe and Dane.

They have a frigging date?

"No!" Zoe interrupted. "I work for him."

Osborne smiled like a cop.

"Your boss comes over at this hour and walks in unannounced?"

It was a rude, arrogant smile.

Flashing red lights spun through Zoe's windows and tires crunched her drive.

"It's the IIPD, Dane," Osborne told him. "Zoe's had a break in."

"You what? Is that why he's here? Are you hurt?"

"I'm not hurt." Zoe looked to the ceiling, around, and back to him. "I don't know when it happened, honestly. It could have been anytime within the past three days."

"Your folks, now this? What are the chances of getting you to stay with Raine? Willow might need some help with Chloe. Better yet, stay at my place. I can sleep on the couch." She turned three shades of red, but she didn't answer him. The hell if he could figure out this woman.

Dane sat with Lucky at an outside table at Show Me's. It was supposed to be a quick lunch, but nothing was quick when it came to Lucky. Not quick or without a reason that would pertain to Lucky and only Lucky.

Dane didn't eat here often, but he swore every time he did, Blake Eaton had moved his outdoor seating further onto the beach. Large tile squares, set on the sand, were covered with plastic, white tables that sat four each. For the price of the food, Dane thought Eaton should spring for better seats, but it wasn't Dane's business.

The restaurant sat at the opposite end of the Island from Sun Trips. It was a favorite of the tourists, especially at sunset. Not many cared about getting sand in their shoes when they could eat with the gulf breeze and sounds of the waves providing nature's best background music.

"You can't stay holed up in this fucking prison much longer, buddy. You'll lose your touch." Six empty bottles sat in front of a large pile of shrimp skins. Lucky peeled them—heads, legs, and all—in one, swift motion, downing each enormous shrimp in one bite.

Facing the beach, Dane propped his feet on the nearest empty chair. "I've got some things to take care of."

"There's nothing left in the Gulf, dumbass. And even if there was, the state's got this water locked up so tight, you'd never get a penny."

Dane flagged their waitress, asking for their ticket as Lucky ordered another Corona.

"You're not going soft on me, are you?" Lucky asked as the waitress cleared his empties. "That sweet spot outside of Australia has more possibilities than a hundred-dollar whore. Come on, man. Days of diving and getting rich, nights of getting laid."

The shorebirds ran in and out with the waves, eating what they could before the water caught them. It was a dance between animal and water and made Dane think of dancing with Zoe.

"This wouldn't have anything to do with a cute little brunette gift shop cashier, would it?" Lucky asked as he rubbed a shrimp around in the beer sauce that oozed on his plate.

It was complicated. Lucky wouldn't understand. "It's good to see you, man, but I've got some things. Go without me."

"What the fuck, Corbin? We've been talking about that spot for years, man. What's up with you? You pussy whipped? Need permission?"

"Fuck you. I go where I please."

Lucky leaned back and took a long swig from his fresh beer. His eyes squinted as he slouched down in his chair. "You're onto something local."

Dane shook his head. "You're drunk, Lucky. You already said it. The state's got these waters tied up tighter than a docking pier in a hurricane."

"Never stopped you before."

A commotion broke out just north of them. Children squealed and half-cocked adults whooped. Then, he saw it. It happened every so often. A full-grown female loggerhead crawled its straight line from the water to deep up the beach. Shit. They were supposed to do this at night.

No one grows up on Ibis Island without knowing what to do when a turtle crawls up to lay its eggs in broad daylight. He had Ibis Island Turtle Conservation on speed dial. Which really just meant Raine's cell. She was the Principal Permit Holder for the island. In theory, she ran this beach.

She answered on the first ring. "Raine Clearwater."

"It's Dane. You've got a girl crawling up on the beach just north of Show Me's."

"Shit. I'm at the other end of the island. Get the people away from her. I'll call Zoe."

"Hello, folks!" He yelled as he jogged over to them. "I'm part of Island Turtle Patrol," he lied. It amused him the way people backed off when he used that title. He wanted to threaten them with his 9mm police issue bucket if they moved a muscle.

"What a treat we have today. Would you look at her? Now,

let's all give her some room. Further, now. That's it. Keep going." He would have preferred they kept going all the way back to their condos, so he could plop down next to her and watch. But tourists were completely mesmerized with sea turtles, and who wasn't? So instead, he kept his eyes on the people, doing his best to keep the creeping feet of the crowd from getting in her way. "She might crawl pretty far, there. So, leave some headway. If we give her room, she might just lay some eggs for us."

The turtle maneuvered her flippers along the sand. Possibly, this could be her first time on land in thirty-some years.

He waved his arms and stepped in front of the few parents with unruly children. Zoe arrived on the scene not five minutes behind him. She had the t-shirt that actually read, 'Island Turtle Patrol' on the front and back. The first thing she did was assess the situation. Her expression said she approved. Kudos for him.

The second was to look at him and frown. "What are you wearing?" she asked.

Wearing? It was embarrassing when she asked it like that. He had on a pair of pants, loafers and linen shirt. "I'm working on my professional look."

"You look better in your leather necklace and khaki shorts." She turned around and dug her knees in the sand in front of the group.

He had no idea why, but it was the nicest compliment/cut-down he could remember getting. He hated wearing this shit. If he admitted it, it was because of seeing the frigging realtor, Richard Beckett, and definitely the detective with their date-that-night bullshit.

He sat back with Lucky who had switched to whiskey on ice by this time. They watched as Zoe animatedly distracted the group away from the turtle.

She pulled out some of the tiny wooden sea turtle tokens she carried with her everywhere she went and wrote on them with magic marker before passing them out to the children. The distraction was perfect.

As he watched her with all those people around her, his mind wandered to the break in. Nothing had come of it. Zoe said she noticed someone had looked through her things but swore nothing was taken. Each year the island became more and more of a tourist destination. More strangers. More rentals built where he swore nothing else could fit. The Clearwaters had better get used to changing with the times and locking their windows and doors.

Their waitress came with their check. "Isn't it fun?" she commented as she nodded her head toward the commotion. "Those tortoises bring us so much business. In July, when the babies start coming out of the ground, our boss says our lights draw them to us so the customers can pick them up. They are the cutest things you've ever seen."

Oh boy. He cringed at the thought of Raine's reaction when he told her this. And he *would* tell her. It made him remember her comment about the lights she'd come out here to check the other week. Ducking his head under them, he saw. No turtle-friendly amber bulbs, no cover for the tops of each, and they weren't pointing toward the restaurant but outward. What a prick.

Dane paid their bill and left before the commotion was over, although he would have preferred acting as one of the tourists, listening to Zoe's impromptu presentation. His draw to Zoe Clearwater seemed to get stronger every day. The date-that-night thing was a problem, and he needed to do something about it. Except what right did he have? Did he ever ask her out? Really ask her, not pretend by cornering her on one of his boats or making a joke about dating the help?

He needed a plan.

NINE

Matt was a nice guy, Zoe reminded herself. He was attractive. He was smart, caring, and a grown up. A grown up who was an adult in more ways than just the date on his birth certificate. It was nice. There was that word again. Nice. She blamed it on her sex moratorium. Her mother was right. It wasn't healthy. She could fix that problem. Maybe even that night. Yeah, right.

They were driving to her parents' restaurant in his four-door sedan. Right up her alley. It was a Fusion. Not an obnoxious turquoise blue off-road vehicle, yet not a car that screamed, 'I live with my mother.' Zoe had been two full hours late, but it hadn't seemed to bother Matt.

Raine had called her in for an emergency. And if Raine called Zoe, it was a big emergency. Willow held more sea turtle conservation permits than Zoe did. Zoe still needed to take the classes on handling the eggs, the one for nest relocations and nest excavations, and the class for handling the hatchlings. But if Willow was working, Raine called Zoe.

It had been an adult male green turtle that the Coast Guard

noticed bobbing irrationally. Greens were highly endangered, even more so than loggerheads, and Zoe wasn't about to let the little guy down. That is, the three hundred pound little guy.

The Coast Guard driver had hauled it into the back of Raine's truck, and she and Zoe drove it all the way to the Aquarium. The biologists thanked them, and Raine kept the small talk small so Zoe could get back in time to rinse the turtle smell off of her before her date.

Matt picked her up at her house like a nice—like a gentleman. "This is my parents' restaurant," Zoe said as they entered the parking lot. "My sister, Willow, works here." She remembered his mention of kissing her after dinner. Where were the butterflies of anticipation? She was turning into a prude.

"I know," he said politely.

"You know this is my parents' restaurant. You knew about the break in at my parents' home. You must be a detective."

It made him laugh. He had a great smile and a better laugh. This was turning out to be more than she expected.

They sat outside. The solid hardwood floor had a bleached tint to it. Her father said it was pickled. Her mother insisted on the linen napkins and china during dinner hours. The fresh flowers on the tables topped the atmosphere, and the amazing food made the cost worth it.

"Did you know the restaurant is called the Beachfront because when it was built, there was nothing between here and the beach?" She gestured over the white painted handrail toward the houses across the street.

"That I did not know."

"Since then, all the tree-themed streets were built; Palm Street, Pine Street, Beech Street. And then, all the rentals that line them. They're damaging the structure of the beach. Which is why the city agreed to allow the government to come in for beach restoration. Most realtors have been good about informing renters to stay off the sea oats and grasses that keep the sand from erosion…and I'm rambling."

"It's interesting. I guess we're too populated at St. Petersburg for much of this."

Willow arrived and plopped right down with them. "Phew." She wiped her forehead more due to theatrics than sweat. "Busy night. In fact, didn't you say you're planning to hit Show Me's after this?"

"I didn't say that," Zoe said, although they had, in fact, discussed it.

"It's the spot you always go. You know, the six times a year we get you out."

Yeah, because Willow never wanted to go to her place.

"Don't you have a restaurant to host?" Shoo fly.

"I'm just sayin'. I think you should hit my place. The addition is coming along nicely. It's gorgeous."

"Have you been drinking?"

"Me? Of course not. But here, let me take your empties and get you a third round. It's on me."

Zoe's second beer had only been half empty.

Three beers down—or maybe two and a half—and Zoe's lightweight self had a buzz going. Which was good, because it was officially after dinner and she truly needed to get the kissing thing out of the way.

She turned down his offer to get the car and pick her up. It was less than a block away. He held out his elbow, inviting her to curl her arm in his. How nice. Offering, but not pushing. She accepted and found it served as a stabilizer to her lightweight self's balance.

When they got to his car, he walked her to the passenger side and unlocked the door. She'd had enough. As he tried to open it for her—nice again—she plopped her butt against it and crossed her arms.

He lifted his brows and smiled. Nice smile.

She looked up to him. Way up. "You're tall."

"True."

Still nothing.

Shrugging, she grabbed him by the shirt and pulled him down. He put his hands on her shoulders as their lips met. He closed his eyes. She wasn't about to. His lips were warm and nice. In an effort to improve this, she turned her head for a better angle. Nothing.

He pulled away first and half-squinted one eye before asking. "So, what do you think?"

Who asked what a person thought after he kissed her?

"It was nice." An honest statement.

"I thought so."

"What's that supposed to mean?"

"I like you."

Uh oh.

"Don't look like that. I really like you. I can talk to you. You're smart. You know a lot about things I don't and enough about what I'm interested in I could talk to you for hours."

"You have but face."

"Excuse me?"

"You're about to say, 'but'."

His expression said she was right. "The kiss."

"It wasn't there."

"It was nice," he repeated.

"I know!" she couldn't believe he used the word. "But it wasn't—"

"Exactly. It wasn't."

"Should we call it a night?" she asked. This should feel

awkward. It should be awkward, but she wasn't feeling that either.

"I'd really like to talk some more and another beer sounds even better."

"Friends?"

He held out his hand, they shook on it, and he opened the car door for her.

Dane called Willow's cell for the third time. He'd waited at the bar for two hours before graduating to the parking lot. "They're not here yet. I ran out of things to talk about with the bartender."

"I'm in the middle of clean up, Dane. They just left."

"Are you sure they're coming here?"

"No. I told them what you wanted me to say. And I'm a terrible liar. She'll know something's up."

"As long as she shows up. How did they look at dinner?"

"The same as the last time you called. Happy. Friendly. Not flirty."

"They're here. I owe you. Bye." He hung up and staged himself against his Jeep. He'd made sure not to park in new car parking so he was mostly in front of the entrance to Luciana's.

She didn't seem to notice when they pulled in the lot. It killed him not to follow Osborne's geek car to the spot where he parked. Which was in new car parking. What if they were making out before they got out of the car? A twitch started in the leg that wasn't holding up his body weight. He'd give them ten more seconds…tops.

They came toward the front door first thing. They weren't touching. She noticed him almost immediately. He pushed away and made his way to them.

"Babe." He refused to be intimidated by a six-foot-two cop. Maybe six-foot-three. "I need to talk to you."

"Hello to you, too, *boss*."

Dane turned his eyes to Osborne, then back to Zoe.

"Would you like some privacy?" Osborne asked.

Dane and Zoe answered in tandem. He saying, "Yes," and she, "No."

"You can say whatever you have to say in front of Matt," she added and stuck her arm in his.

"I don't like this." It wasn't the way he planned to start.

"There are a half-dozen bars on the island then, Dane. Pick one."

Osborne butted in, "I don't think that's what he meant."

Dane took her hand and pulled her away from Osborne, whispering in her ear. "I don't think he's right for you."

"How is that any of your business?" she asked, raising her voice.

There wasn't another person alive who could make him tongue-tied. Damned woman. "Let me start over."

She pulled her arm from him and turned away.

"Please."

The plea made her pull her chin back.

"I know this is bad timing, but I want you...I mean, I'm interested in you. I want to see you. Date you. You know what I mean."

"We've talked about this already."

"No we haven't." He looked to Osborne who was much too calm about the conversation. "We've joked, we've flirted." He put up a finger as she opened her mouth to protest. "We've flirted. I'm serious, now. I don't want you to see this guy." He looked straight at Osborne this time and said, "No offense."

"None taken. I sort of got this when you showed up in her living room."

Confusing dude. Regardless, he tried to lower his voice. "I know you've had a hard couple of years. You're not as weak as you think you are. You swindled me out of load of cash—"

"—you offered—"

"I'm not finished. You sold your business. It was understandable, but you didn't quit. You're still giving tours. So what if you're not diving with groups? Yet. You've poured yourself into the island's turtle conservation."

"I'm going to go on in and get a beer," Osborne interrupted, but by that time neither of them paid much attention.

A tear spilled over her wonderful cheeks.

"You miss your brother. But you don't sit in the house you paid off from the sale of Sun Trips. You work to find answers. You're the most beautiful, smart, sassy woman I know and, I want to date you."

Her shoulders fell as the tears dropped freely, now, breaking his heart into a million pieces. "I'm sorry. Never mind. I didn't mean to—"

But she grabbed the sides of his face and pulled him down to her. Her lips were warm and desperate. His heart reacted long before his head. He dove in, braiding his hands in all of her thick, blonde hair. Her lips were moist and firm. Parting them, he found the taste of her was like opening a deeply hidden shipwreck to find the best treasure of his life. Her arms wrapped around his sides, digging into the muscles in his back as she rotated against his Jeep and yanked him against her.

One of her knees lifted and she propped her boot against a tire, twining her warm legs with his and pressing her female shape into him. Her lips moved and their tongues meshed. It was so much like their dance, intensely sensual and needy. Small sounds came from deep in her throat that, for the first time in his life, made his knees weak. Zoe Clearwater. Goddess of the sea. In his arms. He would never let go.

"Oh gross. Really?"

They came up for air as if they'd run a marathon. Darting their eyes to the direction of the voice, he saw it was Raine. Of course.

"Great timing, Clearwater." He could spit. "What are you doing here?"

"Willow's meeting me. You?"

"Willow?" Zoe asked, still a little breathless as she looked him in the eye.

He smiled and added for Raine's sake, "Yeah, Zoe's date is inside. We'll be there in a minute."

"Get a room or come in. Your choice." She shrugged before adding another, "gross."

"This can't work," Zoe said flatly.

"Yes, it can."

She shook her head. "You're impossible."

A smile spread across his face.

"Oh, and the kiss? It wasn't nice."

Why did he know that was a compliment?

TEN

Dane ached to toss Zoe over his shoulder and drag her off to the nearest cave. Except she had a date. He pulled at the back of her shirt before they got all the way in to Willow's bar. It was crowded, but he spotted Raine sitting alone at a table, drinking from a bottle of Heineken and checking her phone.

Willow's bar was a one-of-a-kind. Other than the no-dancing, it was Dane's pick as his place to kick back. Maybe just not when Osborne sat at the bar downing what looked like a whiskey and coke. She named it Luciana's since it was a near replica of the type of ship Luciana Bezan's Spaniard lover used when he sailed to pick up his Cuban Luciana. As a professional treasure hunter who dove his share of ships, Dane had to hand it to her. Not many patrons would respect the accuracy of the detail.

A few dozen tightly-fitted tables scattered around the long wooden bar. Zoe's brother helped Willow create the ship-cabin booths along the wall and weathered-wood floor. Planks lined the walls with oversized portholes serving as the windows. Thick, braided ropes dangled from the ceiling and worn metal deck tools hung on the walls.

It was an island bar, which meant no food along with the no-dancing. Unless you count bowls of in-the-shell peanuts as food, or wiggling by the jukebox as dancing. Willow was working on both. Since Liam had the summer off of his teaching job, she'd hired him to work on the addition when he wasn't working for Sun Trips.

Zoe must have sensed his reason for tugging at her shirt, because she whispered out of the corner of her mouth. "It's okay. Matt and I have an understanding."

"What are you talking about?"

"When we kissed, we decided we just want to be friends. He's a good guy."

Dane took her arm and spun her all the way around this time. "You kissed Osborne?"

She should be embarrassed or at least act like she was sorry. Instead she just shrugged.

"Tonight?"

Another shrug topped with a grin.

"With the mouth that just kissed me?"

Her shoulders shook as she laughed. Damned woman.

"Do you need to brush your teeth?" she asked. "I have some gum if you'd like."

"Just keep walking."

They headed for the bar. It didn't seem like Raine noticed them since she didn't take her eyes from her phone, but she must've, because she got up and started toward them.

"I'm sorry we took so long," Zoe told Osborne as if nothing happened. "Miller Lite, please, Paula. We've got a good crowd tonight."

"Paula?" Osborne asked. "No Luciana?"

"No," Zoe answered him like they were new best friends. "Willow is the owner. Paula is head bartender. Luciana is a local legend. She was the daughter of a one of the many poor Cuban families who came into money from farming. Legend has it that a rich Spaniard fell in love with her. She had a dowry equipped with solid gold toilet basins, pure silver candlesticks and jewel-encrusted weapons. He was on his way back to Mexico with her and her dowry when his disapproving family attacked and sunk the ship."

Osborne glanced around as she explained. "Wow. Cheers to Willow." He drank the last sip from his mixed drink. "Did you get everything straightened out?" Osborne asked, gesturing his head toward the parking lot door as if Dane wasn't standing right next to them.

There it was. The red started at her neck and made it all the way through her cheeks. It gave Dane a sudden need to beat his chest.

"Raine," Zoe nearly yelled as she changed the subject. "This is Matt, the detective I was telling you about."

She told Raine about him? His silverback gorilla era was frigging short-lived.

"The cop." Raine said as a flat statement.

"Don't mind her," Zoe said. "She doesn't get along so well with law enforcement."

"We have police on Ibis Island?" Raine asked. "I'll be damned."

"It's true," Zoe defended her. "They don't show themselves around many places other than city board meetings."

"That reminds me," Dane said to Raine. "Show Me's hasn't changed their lights since the last time we were there." He contemplated how to get around the second part. "Now, don't go flying off the handle, but one of his waitresses made it sound as if he likes his lights the way they are, because they draw the turtle hatchlings to the customers so they can handle them close and personal."

"That bastard." She slammed her empty bottle on the bar making Osborne jump. What a wimp.

"I knew it," Raine growled. "I've got a mind to take a BB gun to each one of his precious little code violation lights."

"Except that you just said all that in front of a cop." Dane metaphorically patted himself on the back for saying so since he might not mind watching Raine cuffed and booked, if only for one night.

"I'm almost afraid to ask," Osborne cowered. "But why is it bad to handle the turtle hatchlings?"

Raine's expression softened at his interest. "They are an endangered species and protected by federal and state law. You need to be trained and licensed to handle sea turtles, young or old. Only one in a thousand make it to sexual maturity. They don't need to be taking field trips to Show Me's on their way to the water. Your date, here, isn't even trained to handle the turtles."

Raine saw Dane and Zoe lip-locked in the parking lot. She said that last part to spite him. And after he just ratted out the Show Me's owner for her. Some gratitude.

"If it's a code violation, you could call the code violation officer," Osborne suggested.

"I'm not sure our code violation officer has ever issued a code violation," Zoe added.

"Not one?"

Raine looked him dead on. "Not a single damned freaking one."

The door opened and Willow breezed in. She did a walk through, then asked Paula for an amaretto stone sour. "Look at all of us, here and cozy," she said overzealously. She was right; she sucked at lying.

"How do you look so fresh after running a restaurant for six hours straight?" Raine asked her.

"Yoga on the beach. Pilates, and lavender baths. Hello again, Matt."

"You two know each other?" Raine gestured between Willow and Osborne with the next beer Paula had handed her.

Willow would keep his secret even if she sucked at it. "They ate at Beachfront tonight. Grilled grouper," she pointed to Zoe, "And fried grouper," pointing to Osborne. "Both excellent choices."

Dane definitely did not need to know what they ordered.

"Any news on the skull?" Willow asked.

Three sets of female Clearwater eyes all drilled Osborne. Dane almost felt sorry for the dude, but then no.

Osborne picked up the glass of water he'd changed to. "Sure. The St. Petersburg Times should have it out on Monday in the police report section. Forensics concluded the skull belonged to a male, approximately twenty-eight to thirty-two years old. From the looks of the crustaceans on it and the knife, the sea scrubs think it's been down there for at least a year."

Dane's eyes darted to Zoe first. Her brows dropped low as she stared at Osborne, but healthy color stayed in her face. He moved his glance to her sisters. Willow stared at the bar.

"Am I the only one awake, here?" Raine asked.

Zoe laughed a half-breath, but her smile didn't reach her eyes. "Are you serious, Raine?"

Raine sighed and closed her eyes. "It is a stretch." She shook her head. "But what if?"

The tension in Zoe's shoulders might not be noticed by someone like Osborne, but Dane noticed. He didn't care who saw or where any relationship between he and Zoe stood, there was no stopping his arms from wrapping around from the back of her to her waist. As natural as the sea, she took his arms and wrapped them tighter like she was standing in a cool December breeze.

Osborne cleared his throat, then rubbed the back of his neck. What he needed to do was get the hell out of their personal business. "I, uh, meant to ask you about that tonight." He was looking straight at Zoe, now, and made Dane's jaws clench and release.

"It might, uh, not hurt to check it out."

This did make Zoe shiver, every piece of her. "As if what, Matt? The skull is my brother?"

"Zoe." Raine's voice was uncharacteristically soft. She placed the tips of her fingers on Zoe's forearm.

Zoe jerked away from her touch. Dane held on tighter. "You think Seth could have somehow been involved in…" Her voice shook with her body. "Have been in a situation where…could have been…" She couldn't say the word. None of them could.

Ignoring Zoe, Willow whispered almost inaudibly to Osborne. "We have hair clippings. Hair clippings and baby teeth."

Zoe stood for a long time at the beach access. It was the one with easy parking at the end of Pine Street. Tall Jessamine lined one side and thick sea oats the other. When she was ready, she took off her sandals and set them beside the bench at the opening. Flags and iPad in hand, she began the methodical work of her morning patrol. It was dark, but tracks from any three hundred pound female sea turtle would be easy to spot in the light colored sand.

Her beach-patrol days were Mondays, Fridays, and Saturdays. She was a 'walker.'

Her business had taken too much of her time to become a coordinator like Willow and certainly not the Primary Permit Holder. That position had been practically handmade for Raine.

When Zoe owned Sun Trips Touring, she volunteered to walk this section of the beach on Mondays only. It was the slowest day for tourists. As time went on, volunteers had to quit, one to take care of an ill mother and another to join Seth in the great waters beyond.

Seth. The waiting would kill her.

It didn't seem to be killing her mother, though. She'd been like a rock taking the news, the possibilities, giving up the hair and tooth from their sacred spots in his mementos. She didn't demand to see the photo of the skull. No hysterics. She stood like a mother, reassuring the children she still had left. "Seth has moved on. He doesn't live in any skull," she'd said through a smile as the steady stream of tears ran down her face.

The sand massaged the bottom of Zoe's feet as she walked alone the beating waves breaking the monotony.

It had occurred to Zoe how much her mother and Willow were the rocks. Everyone thought Raine was the strong one, but it wasn't true. Raine was organized, assertive, and an essential part of their family and this island. But her mother and Willow, they had an inner peace that produced a strength beyond will alone and certainly not found in Zoe.

She felt her shoulders fall as she strolled, checking for tracks as she went. She was like them...the volunteers. So many came to the island for just this, the sea turtles. The depressed, alcohol addicted, those who suffered PTSD, hermits. They came and generally conquered their ball and chain. The elderly section three coordinator showed up after losing everything; his wife, his job, his retirement. He had been a recluse, barely surviving on his social security check before he signed up for Ibis Island Turtle Conservation. Now, he was a new man. Never missed his mornings, and took all the tests to become a section coordinator.

Her feet stopped, a sudden wave of sadness rushing over her. Taking a deep breath of sea air, she closed her eyes.

No. She was projecting. Dane's cobalt blue eyes stared at her from behind her eyelids. They were intense yet full of warmth. He believed in her. 'You didn't quit,' he'd said. 'You keep looking for answers.'

Her chin lifted. She turned to face the breeze head on, letting the air blow her hair behind her. She opened her eyes with a jolt. Turning her head, she saw him. His sandy hair whipped around his face. Khaki shorts, a Sun Trips polo, and bare feet. She smiled, wondering at which beach access he left his shoes.

He watched her but didn't move. Dane Corbin. Traveler. Playboy. Friend. Confidant. She trusted him. He'd earned it, she had to admit. She also had to acknowledge their chemistry. No, it wasn't nice. It sent the world around her spinning like she was in the center of a hurricane. The churning water around her was her life and somehow they had become the calm in the center.

Her feet moved toward him before her head had a chance to tell them not to. "It's five a.m.," she said just loud enough for him to hear over the wind.

"I knew you'd be out here. Beautiful morning." He wasn't looking at the scenery.

"You don't need to be here."

"You said we should be discreet. This is discreet," he said, lifting his arms to the empty beach.

"It is." She laced her fingers in his hand and they turned south. His were thick and strong from years of working on boats and searching for buried treasure. The connection was natural, too natural.

She spotted tracks ahead. "Look." She pointed and caught when his gaze landed on the row of adult turtle tracks making a perpendicular line from the water's edge inland.

"Loggerhead," she said when they got closer.

"Why?"

"I think of loggerhead tracks as swimming freestyle over the sand. A green's tracks look more like a butterfly stroke. See?" With Dane's history of college swimming, she knew the comparison wouldn't be lost on him. She pointed out the deep alternating grooves left in the sand from the girl's huge flippers.

The tracks led to a spot inland. She turned around, judged where the turtle stopped and turned before scooting back to the water.

"This is fun." He ran his hand down the length of her arm. "Do we get out the stakes and mark it?"

She shook her head. "False crawl. Look, there's no bowl, no round shaped divot or evidence of sand thrown to cover a nest. She must have changed her mind." Zoe needed to record it anyway. She stuck a flag at the end of the tracks for the coordinator. Taking her iPad, she filled out the data form Raine would need to report to the state.

Taking his hand, she moved further down the beach. "I think it's tied into the break in at my folks' house. And mine."

No need to spell out her change in subject for him.

"You don't know if it's Seth yet," he qualified. "Osborne said a few weeks."

She shook her head as if that might clear the possibility. "I don't think it's Seth."

He sighed. She could hear it over the waves and the wind.

"Regardless of whether it is Seth or not, think about it. I find the skull. Word travels around this island like a quick moving storm. My parents' home is broken into. The person chose Seth's old room. The drawers of his dresser were open. Then, my house. The house of the one who found the skull. Someone wants to find out if I know anything, maybe if Seth had something to hide." She shook her head more forcefully.

His fingers tightened around her hand, slowly, a small squeeze at a time.

"Dane?"

"Oh shit. Sorry." He loosened his grip. "You're making too much sense." He stopped and turned her to face him.

A tear had dripped over her lower lid. Of the few traits she inherited from her mother, the tears were one she could have done without. He used his thumb to brush it away and spread his fingers across her cheek, then in her hair. Her lids closed as her muscles loosened. She hadn't realized how tight they were.

His lips touched hers, sending the same tsunami through her body as they had in the parking lot over the weekend. Want, need. This time it was more emotion and less primal. Peace, sensations. She dropped her flags and iPad in the sand and slithered her hands around his back, exploring, learning.

ELEVEN

What was she doing? Zoe didn't care. This was right. Their lips moved together as if they'd done this for years. It was much like their dance. They fit, moving together... familiar, yet new. His hands laced through her hair, then grasped. She didn't want to ever move from this spot.

His knee dipped between hers, inching their bodies closer as he released her mouth. His warm lips traveled a slow trek across her jaw to her neck, finding the sensitive spot just behind her ear. A small moan betrayed her. She tilted her head, inviting him in, and opened her eyes in response to her undoing.

"Dane!" She pushed him away, put her free hand on his shoulder, and turned his body south. "Look."

A large female crawled out of the gulf like a giant creature from a horror movie. She maneuvered her flippers across the sand as instinct moved her forward.

"Holy shit," Dane whispered. "Look at that."

She barely had time to pick up her iPad before he grabbed her hand and took off down the beach. It was a green. "Wait 'til Raine finds out about this one."

"Mother fucker, she's a giant."

Ha. Dane was careful not to drop the f-bomb around her. His eyes lit up like he'd just found Luciana's Dowry.

"How much do you think she weighs? Is this one going to lay eggs? I've never seen this when there weren't a few dozen tourists around that needed to be tamed."

Guys loved this stuff. Always faking disinterest until they were in the midst of it, then they couldn't contain their interest. It was good to know Dane was a human male. "Around four hundred pounds, and let's hope she lays her eggs. We'll keep our distance until she's about done digging."

"She looks like a beached whale, inching along by her fins."

"I expect she feels like a beached whale, especially with all those eggs in her. Greens are always this big. They lay between 100 and 150 eggs. But it's early in the season. She'll save the sperm inside her for a few more nests."

"What fun is that?" It sounded a bit too much like playboy Dane to her.

They sat a few yards away and watched it find a spot. It turned, creating a shallow, oval divot in the sand.

"She picked a spot next to some sea oats. That's good and bad."

Without taking his eyes from the turtle, he maneuvered his way behind Zoe, sticking his legs out so she was sandwiched between them. His body was warm and firm. Thick arms wrapped around her and stubble brushed her cheek. It was like the f-bomb he dropped. His movements were subconscious.

Watching the female dig her nest was as exciting as the first time. The scene lifted much of the weight pressing on her shoulders from the distant possibility that the skull might belong to Seth. From Dane's reactions, she was certain this truly was his first time up and personal.

"The good is that since the sea oats are a protected species, the nest will be away from tourist activity. The bad is that some of the hatchlings will get tangled in the roots. Federal regulations require nest excavation seven days after the hatchlings emerge. Raine or Willow will likely find some live ones when they do."

"Why not Zoe?" he asked as he took off her hat and laid it on the ground next to them. She couldn't possibly be expected to have a coherent conversation when Dane Corbin was stroking her hair over her shoulder and down her back.

"I don't have an excavation permit." She shivered.

"Why the hell not? No, don't tell me. How do you get an exhuming permit?"

"Excavation permit." Zoe sighed. When she had her business, she told herself she didn't have time. Now, she simply didn't trust herself enough to handle the responsibility. "And I'd have to take a class. Raine won't give any certification classes until after season. It's okay. They let me watch."

"We'll see about that. I want to do that thing where I buy the nest."

The female turned just enough to fling sand on their feet. Dane ran his hands down the length of Zoe's arms, grabbing her wrists and wrapping them around her. What was his question? Oh. "You can't buy a nest. You can adopt a nest."

"Yeah, that's it. What is that again?"

"A wooden plaque in the shape of a sea turtle with your name on it is staked in front of the nest."

He rotated his head and bit her earlobe. It sent a shiver of lust through her body making her pitifully weak.

"When the nest hatches, you'll be mailed the weathered plaque, the data about the nest and some other cool stuff."

"Can I have this one?" he whispered.

She'd see to it herself if he would just keep doing what he was doing to her ear. "I think I can pull some strings."

The green dipped her tail end into a yard-deep hole. "Now

we can get closer." Slowly, they moved around the back of her and leaned over the hole. They were shoulder-to-shoulder, now, with their hands on their thighs. One ping-pong ball sized white egg after another dropped. She couldn't help it and started counting in her head.

"Aren't they breaking? That's a long frigging way down."

She couldn't count and answer at the same time. It was a shame, since his excitement was contagious. Instead, she smiled and whispered, "Sixteen, seventeen, eighteen."

She ended at one hundred twenty-nine but missed some in the beginning.

"They don't break, no. The shells are pliable and leathery. I don't have the permit that allows me to touch the eggs, either. That's a nest relocation permit."

She sensed he was looking at her and not the green, so she turned her head and found him squinting, brows dug low.

"Look."

The green started pushing sand in the hole. Zoe had to admit, she too was surprised the eggs didn't break from the massive weight of the turtle as it packed the sand on the nest.

Dane stood and linked fingers with Zoe. It felt comfortable, much too comfortable. What the hell was she doing?

"Wow," he said as the turtle waddled back to the water. "That is some crazy shit. I feel like I need a cigarette after a long night of sex."

And at that, she remembered exactly why she shouldn't be doing what the hell she was doing.

She didn't tell Dane she was going to St. Petersburg. It was for the better. She was sure of it. Almost. Nearly subconsciously, she chose her playlist with *Welcome to the Jungle* and *Sweet Child O' Mine* and cranked it.

The drive north helped. The Skyhigh bridge. The long stretches with miles of water on both sides. Occasional rows of palm trees. Nothing could quite clear her mind like the scent of a crisp gulf breeze.

Dane Corbin.

Why couldn't she date him for a while? It would be a nice distraction to the horrible waiting about the skull. It didn't have to be a serious thing, certainly not exclusive. They were easy around each other. With him, it was like riding a bike, no planning ahead what to say, no awkward silence that needed to be filled with small talk. They had chemistry. She felt the heat roll up her neck and over her face as she let their dance brush through her memory. She had no doubt he could absolutely make a break in her sex moratorium one to remember.

She couldn't date him for the same reason she could.

Because he was Dane Corbin. He probably had some girl at his house right then, smoking a cigarette after some long night of sex. She gripped the steering wheel until her knuckles turned white.

He was confident, right with who he was, didn't need to answer to anyone or commit to anyone. He had the nerve to get up and go on month-long treasure-hunting adventures at the drop of a hat. And he could take the time to bring an oxygen tank to an employee who treated him like he had the plague.

She almost missed the freaking exit again. Her heart was heavy for more reasons than Dane. The days-old newspaper that was secured in her glove box weighed on her heart. She hoped Matt would listen to her.

She parked far from the door, then kicked herself for doing so. The receptionist was a woman this time, dressed in the same police uniform as the others. A numbness came over her. She worked to forget about Dane Corbin and to focus on reality. Using the meditative breathing her parents taught her, she waited patiently in the comfortable seats.

Matt didn't tell the receptionist to have her meet him upstairs. He came to the lobby and greeted her with a handshake before pulling her in for a one-armed hug. "Come. We can talk upstairs."

His office looked like it belonged to someone who worked hard. Stacks of papers in neat piles on his desk, two boxes she assumed held evidence for some case or another. Framed diplomas and certificates hung all along the walls. He'd had a lot of training. From many places. She wondered how he ended up in Florida.

"I assume you're here about the skull," he said as he sat.

She followed his lead, sinking into one of the two guest chairs that sat across from his large, wooden desk. Her words stuck in her throat, so she nodded her response.

He leaned back in his chair. "I've never been through anything like you have. My family is intact and safe and sound in Nevada. I won't try and tell you I understand."

"The break-ins."

His chest rose and fell slowly. "Did you think of something new? Do you remember a face?"

"I wish," she sighed. "Don't you think the break-ins are a bit too much of a coincidence?"

"I think it's a big ocean out there."

She assumed he was being both literal and metaphorical. "Gulf."

"Gulf, right. It's a big Gulf and a lot of miles of coast and caverns. The possibilities are endless. As much as I can't imagine how hard it is for you to wait, it's the sensible choice, waiting. Have you thought of the possibility that you might want this?"

Her eyes jerked to him. How dare he?

"It would be easier. It would bring closure for your family."

"You, you think I somehow want my brother to have been murdered so...so I can somehow be relieved of my part of the responsibility of his disappearance?" If he said it again, she would gladly spend months in jail for scratching his eyes out.

"I just don't want to see you disappointed if it isn't him. It really is a big oc—Gulf out there," he said again.

He wasn't listening. She was nearly ready to storm out without even showing him the newspaper article.

"On the other hand, the break-ins are a stretch for me. Even if the skull isn't your brother's, it seems someone thinks it is. I've talked to Chief Roberts."

He did?

"I'm starting to understand your sister's aversion to anyone in the police force. He's not as...cooperative as I'd hoped. I can't get him to schedule patrols past your house or even your parents'. I had to strong-arm him to give me copies of the files from the original investigation. The best I can do is tell you what I've said before. Keep your windows and doors locked. Don't go anywhere alone. Especially in the dark."

"I'm a beach walker."

"You're a what?"

"I volunteer for Ibis Island Turtle Conservation three times a week. I walk the beach early mornings on those days. It's dark."

"Can't you wait until daylight?"

She could. Then, other people would be walking the beach, ruining her alone time. But since the idea was not to be alone, she could walk the beach later in the morning. "I suppose. For a while, anyway. I found something." Her heart picked up as she said it.

She pulled the newspaper article from her tiny purse. Unfolding it, she scooted forward to the front edge of her seat.

Flattening it out seemed useless, but it occupied her hands, so she tried. Matt's eyes traced the paper, but he waited quietly.

"My father found this. We haven't told my mother. She'll go crazy when she finds out we haven't." She was rambling and realized her hands were shaking. Clasping them together, she continued. "There was a break in at this apartment complex. It's inland about three miles, but that doesn't matter. It says here," she let go of her grip and pointed to the place she'd memorized in the print. "Apartment #4B was broken into. No one was home. Some vandalism was done. A wall broken into. This was where Seth lived before he died."

TWELVE

Dane sat at a table in the outside section of the Clearwater's restaurant. It was mid-week, mid-afternoon. Traffic picked up as the new tourists for the coming weekend trickled onto the island. Down the street were two of the island's accommodations buildings. Cars slowed down, turned around, or pulled over to check a map. Same old, same old.

Most of the time he enjoyed meeting new people from faraway places. Ibis Island was a place people came to relax, kick back, get in some quality diving, and maybe a glimpse of a sea turtle. Not many came to cause beach trouble. It's hard to do that with someone like Raine around.

"Okay. Floors are swept, dishes are done, food is prepped." Willow took the seat next to him with Chloe close on her heels.

"Well, hello, young lady. Have you seen a little six year old girl around here?" Dane asked her. "About yea tall? I didn't expect your mom to bring a young lady to my table."

Chloe blushed like Zoe. Except, she looked like her dad. It had been five years since his death. Dane's eyes turned to Willow who seemed to be thinking the same thing. He took her hand. "You've been working a lot. How are you holding up?"

"I have my Yoga and Pilates. They keep me balanced. And now that its summer, I have my helper here. We're holding up quite well, aren't we, *young lady?*" Willow squeezed his fingers before letting go. He read the tired on her face.

"You need a boat trip. Both of you." He turned to Chloe.

"Oh Mom, can we? When, Mr. Corbin? I mean…if it's okay with my mom." The look on her face was somewhere between pleading and a small threat of a tantrum if Willow said no.

"I'm sorry," he amended. "I should have asked in private."

"We'd love to, actually. On a Monday, I assume? Those are the slow days at both Luciana's and here. I assume they're your slow days, too."

"That's right. Is this Monday too short of notice? I know Liam's been talking about an easy afternoon, too."

"Let's ask Raine and Zoe. We could make it a party."

He nodded. "It's a plan."

"Yesss," Chloe fist-pumped the air. "I'm going to go snorkeling and catch sand dollars. Liam always helps me find sand dollars. And I'm going to work on my tan."

It made him smile. Willow and Chloe were two of his favorite women. Speaking of favorite women. "Zoe clammed up again."

He appreciated the way her expression fell. "But you were making such good progress."

"We were. I don't know what spooked her. I'm not as patient as I thought I'd be."

"Oh, Dane. Throw me a bone, here. I'm female. I need more than that."

"We kissed again. On the beach."

"You kissed Zoe?" Chloe said it like it was a disease.

"Just before a mama sea turtle came up and laid her eggs," he said to Chloe. "And after."

Chloe wrinkled her nose.

"I wish you would let me say something to her."

Willow was a girl. She wouldn't understand. She'd been after him to open up and tell Zoe about the changes he'd made in his life over the past year or so. Well, since the day Zoe came crying on his doorstep, wanting to sell Sun Trips.

Zoe still thought of him as selfish. A womanizer. He'd earned it. "I want her to make her own opinions. And not because her sister told her to." He dropped a large bill on the table. "But thank you. You're a real friend."

"You're welcome, but it's killing me. She cares about you. She wants you more than she knows, but she doesn't see."

"I hope you're right. How about ten Monday morning? Maybe it will take everyone's mind off of your brother. In fact, do you think your parents would come?"

Willow's eyes lit up almost as much as Chloe's who was bopping up and down in her chair. "I'll ask. What a great idea."

"Let me. I haven't seen your mother since the break-in at her house."

Dane parked in front of the Clearwater home, alongside the rows of honeysuckle. The scent reminded him of Zoe. Damned, confusing woman.

The sight of the goats grazing on the roof should have been jarring. Henry Clearwater had been guiding goats up there every day for too many years for it to jar anyone anymore. From this angle, Dane could see the ramp Henry built for them so they could climb up early in the morning and back again at night. He better be glad the police on Ibis Island didn't regulate much of anything.

As he slid down from his Jeep, Harmony came around from

the side of the house carrying a basket. Her face lit when she spotted him. Yes, he adored this woman.

"Dane. It's so lovely to see you. I was just gathering some snap beans for dinner. Are you hungry?"

"I can't stay, thanks. Can I get that for you?"

She smiled and handed him the basket. Together they harvested a half-bushel.

"Summer is here. I won't get much more out of this garden." For the first time Dane could remember, she sounded like an elderly woman.

"I bet you have a pantry full of canned stuff."

She didn't look elderly. The lines that drew from her eyes when she smiled made her look smart and distinguished. Who says that only happens to dudes?

"I think I'll take some of this mint for tea. Surely you have time for some tea?"

"I can do that." He followed her back around the side of the house. A very large mermaid surrounded by goldfish stared down at him as they passed on the stone walkway. "I came by to see if I could talk you into a ride on our newest pontoon boat Monday. Willow and Chloe are coming. So is Liam, and I plan to ask Raine."

"You might want to have Willow ask Raine. My girl can hold a nasty grudge."

"But from as far back as high school?"

"When Seth left for college, she felt it was her job to take over as eldest brother. But no, I don't think that's all of it."

Did he want to ask? He was the one who started the conversation. That's what happens when a guy starts a conversation. "Do you mind me asking what that might be, then? She does have a direct influence on Zoe, and something tells me that you're well aware I'd like to see more of her."

"And she'd like to see more of you, dear. Honey in your tea?"

He sighed. Women were an endless puzzle. Why did he bother? Why couldn't he be more like Henry and worry about keeping quiet and taking care of his goats?

"No honey." He put the basket on the counter and gazed around as she started rinsing the beans under running water. The kitchen hadn't changed much from the few and far between times he'd been in it. Cabinets with glass doors, each framed in white-painted wood. Exposed spice racks and cookie jars in the shapes of pigs and grandmas. He decided to let her take the lead from here.

She filled an old-fashioned teapot with water and started snapping beans. He washed his hands and helped.

"Raine thinks you can't keep it in your pants."

He froze mid-snap. How had he forgotten Harmony's aversion to filtered conversation? It was always funny when the topic was someone other than himself. He was speechless. It was rare but true.

They snapped and rinsed for a few more minutes before Dane built the nerve to ask, "And how would Raine know about my...pants?"

Harmony shrugged. It was a youthful gesture as many of her mannerisms were. "She thinks she knows."

"What do you think?" It was one of those questions that came out before he realized who exactly he was asking.

"I think I know a man in need of a good roll in the hay when I see one."

Great. Man slut to can't-get-a-piece in one quick conversation.

"You should tell Zoe why you haven't been with women lately." She didn't even question her theory.

"I shouldn't have to." It was like talking to Willow. Women. Time for a subject change. "Do you think you'll come out on the boat Monday?"

"We'd love to." Didn't she have to ask Henry or something? "With or without Zoe and Raine."

———

Dane sat with Liam at the end of the bar at Luciana's, drinking glasses of water between shots of tequila. It was Dane's definition of moderation. Lick wrist. Sprinkle salt. Lick salt. Toss back shot. Do not cringe at the burn in front of another dude. Then, suck a lime wedge and pretend the look on your face is from the lime, not the tequila. Pick up glass of water and all is good in the world.

He confessed his conversation with Harmony. It was the tequila's fault. "Even old ladies know I'm not getting any."

Liam laughed. Some friend. "You could always choose the open approach with Zoe and tell her why you're not getting any."

Dane dumped his elbow on the bar and plopped his chin in his hand as he sipped around the salt. "Funny, coming from you."

Not laughing now, was he?

"That's different, asshole."

"It's been five fucking years," Dane slurred.

Liam looked pissed, but he always did when Dane brought up Willow.

"Five years. Isn't that supposed to mean something?" Dane said. "I think it's the friends-don't-date-friends'-ex's expiration date."

"Best friends. Dead friend. Dead, best friend who died in battle."

"Land of the free, baby." Dane lifted his glass and cheered with the air. It wasn't fair, he knew. Somewhere deep inside he knew he was pissed at himself, but it was easier to take it out on Liam.

The door opened and let in a temporary glare from the

streetlights. "Oh hell." It was all three of them. His five shots hadn't done enough to drown out his conversation with Willow. *I wish you would let me say something to her.* Or Harmony, for that matter. *I know a man in need of a good roll in the hay when I see one.* It was definitely easier to be pissed off at Zoe. This was all her fault anyway.

Dane stood when they approached. "The turtle sisters."

"Is that supposed to be an insult, Corbin?" Raine barked as she eyed his empty shot glasses. "It's eight o'clock."

"Hey Raine," Liam said as he stood with Dane. "Willow. Zoe. What gives?"

Willow finished Raine's statement. "You're loaded at eight o'clock in the afternoon."

"Eight o'clock isn't the afternoon," Zoe said to Willow.

Dane didn't want her help. "Don't stand up for me, Zoe."

"Someone might need to stand for you since it doesn't look like you can do it on your own."

She wore a sundress, striped with light blue and yellow. The sandals on her feet had those straps that wound up her ankles. His chest expanded. He forgot to exhale for a few seconds. When he did, it was the kind a guy does when he was defeated.

He didn't care if it was obvious he was looking her over. Or that his chin dropped several inches as his eyes bore into hers. "You and I, babe." He put an emphasis on the word, 'babe.'

"There is no you and I, Dane Corbin. You need some water."

"Oh, there's a you and I, all right." He moved his tired feet purposefully and stepped nose to nose with her.

She didn't back up, not one inch. Damned sexy woman. Damned strong, sexy woman.

THIRTEEN

"You're not kissing me again," Zoe said flatly without flinching.

"I have every intention of kissing you again."

"You kissed Zoe?" It was Liam.

Some friend. Wasn't it in the friend manual that Liam was supposed to wait until later to ask him that? Or maybe the friend manual said Dane was supposed to tell Liam he kissed Zoe before this. Damned, fucking manual.

"Yeah," Raine interrupted. "Kissing might be an understatement for what they were doing. They did it in this very parking lot. A few minutes after she kissed Detective Osborne in Willow's parking lot. Floozy slut."

Zoe rubbed her hands over her beautiful blushing face, then over her hair. "We came by to see about Monday. Don't we—I mean you have a tour scheduled? Or shouldn't you?"

The bartender brought the next shot Dane had ordered.

"I'm the boss." He meant it in more ways than one.

Squinting at him, she picked up his shot, placed it to her lips, and threw it back. She may have shuddered like she'd been in the cold for hours, but she didn't touch the salt or the lime.

The heat between them flowed like waves that came before a tropical storm. Good thing they were in a public place because he could have taken her then and there.

"Henry and Harmony are coming," he said to prove her throwing back that shot hadn't just robbed him of his head and his heart. "And Liam is coming, Willow." Overtly, Dane nudged Liam in the ribs and winked.

Uh, oh.

"Drink anymore tequila, dick head," Liam put an emphasis on the name, "and you'll add another night alone to the months you've already stacked up."

He ratted him out. Liam ratted out Dane's secret. Right in front of Zoe. How could he?

Oh, right. Dane had just ratted him out in front of Willow. What a cluster fuck. Liam didn't deserve it. Before Dane put his foot deeper where it didn't need to be, he pushed his way through the group and staggered outside, pressing the speed dial number he used for the local cab company.

"What the hell is the matter with you?"

Zoe. Just what he didn't need.

He couldn't keep it together with her. Not tonight. Not after his female lecture from Willow followed by the humiliating one from Harmony. Not to mention Liam calling him out in front of all three Clearwater sisters.

He leaned against the weathered wooden siding. Luckily the window next to them was covered in beer posters. He couldn't take another shared moment that included her sisters. She paced in front of him. Her pink painted toes pressed into her sandals each time she rotated. He wasn't sure what she was contemplating, but his thoughts happily stayed on her pink painted toes.

"Months?" she asked.

"Hmm?" Oh.

"Why didn't you tell me you haven't been...ya know? Because of me? Is that true?"

Here it goes again. Willow, Harmony, now—

He didn't have a chance to answer her one way or another, because she threw herself at him. She tasted like tequila and woman. Her honeysuckle scent emptied his last ounce of common sense.

The dress was paper thin. Holy shit, there was no way he could keep it together. Her breasts...absolutely C cups...pressed into him as her hands grabbed and took.

Their lips and tongues were like their dance...forceful and sensual.

In this state of mind, the concrete sidewalk looked like it could serve as a bed. He didn't want to be without this, without her. He had to have her, to keep her.

"Zoe," he said between kisses.

She ignored him and ran the palm of her hand around his side and down the front of his pants.

"Zoe," he said louder and grabbed her hand. "We're in a parking lot."

Her smile was pure evil and sent any leftover bit of common sense away from his months-long neglected pants.

"I want you," she crooned.

Those three little words sucked out every ounce of willpower he had left. They were saved only by the sound of tires crunching through the entrance and turning into one of the parking spots.

Reflexively, Zoe pushed away. The look on her face didn't puzzle him like it usually did. It was a look of trust...of belief. Neither of which she'd ever offered him before. "I can't quit thinking about you," she hummed.

He placed the palm of his hand on the side of her face. Her cheek was warm and smooth, the feel of her hair over his fingertips silky and natural. No crunchy hairspray. No balancing on spiky heels. The dress covered her thighs and cleavage and was sexier than any dress on any woman he had in his memory. "This is too important. I want to do this right. It's too soon for…that." His insides were smacking the hell out of him as he spoke the words.

Her eyelids dropped closed and she turned her beautiful cheek into his hand. He let his thumb travel across her smooth jawline, memorizing the texture.

As the couple from the car approached the front door of Luciana's, he and Zoe pulled away naturally. She smiled at him. No teeth, no sauce. Just a slight smile of acceptance that needed no words.

Everyone was there except Willow. Harmony wore her signature large brimmed hat and wouldn't let Henry carry the wicker basket she brought. It was bigger than a suitcase and made Dane's stomach growl. Always thinking like a Sun Trips captain, Liam checked the fire extinguisher and stacked the extra chairs. Raine had already found a spot in the front and was stripped down to her bikini.

Zoe sat on the picnic table, waiting for Willow who had some Yoga thing she taught on Monday mornings. The two who would run the gift shop that morning were on cleaning duty, one sweeping and the other emptying trash.

Zoe sat uncharacteristically ramrod straight on the table, legs crossed and hands on her knees. One exaggerated sigh later, she slid down, pulling the sack of garbage from the nearest can and tying the ends. Greg stopped to thank her, looked to Dane, looked back to Zoe, then to Lilly who had the broom. The two employees exchanged a look that told him Zoe was right. They do talk. Well, shit. He would have to do something about that.

He appreciated that he could drive the boat wearing nothing but his trunks. Too many more days as a working stiff and he could end up with a golfer's tan.

"All aboard the Sun Trips Touring finest party pontoon. Leave your…uh…pipes in the car, ladies and gentlemen. This is a law-abiding business." Harmony's laugh was contagious. And since it was only ten a.m., they didn't even have beer in the coolers, let alone any fictitious weed.

Willow came running from the parking lot wearing her workout gear. Zoe hugged her, then followed behind. He couldn't see Zoe's eyes under the brim of her cowboy hat. She gave him a wide berth as she stepped onto the boat.

She lifted her head to brush glances with him, then smiled just enough to confuse him. She wouldn't like it if he winked at her with Greg watching, so he refrained and used the textbook speech all Sun Trips captains gave to each tour. "Watch your step, and please take notice of the life jacket, ring, and fire extinguisher. You don't need to know how to use them, just where they're located. Thank you." There was no one on the boat who didn't know the rules. Zoe's proximity was as short lived as her glance. Quickly, she started rummaging through Willow's bag as he taxied away from the pier.

It bothered him that working for him bothered her.

"Please help yourself to the refreshments located in the coolers in both the bow and the back of the boat." He worked on his artificial captain sarcasm. As if any Clearwater would drink out of disposable plastic. "We'll stop at the sandbar closest to The Kitchen so Miss Chloe can get her hands on some starfish." She was the cutest kid he'd ever laid eyes on.

Funny how any mention of either Willow or Chloe brought Dane's mind right to Liam. He sat in the front, ignoring Dane's obnoxious act. Liam may have been talking to Raine, but his focus was on Chloe's reaction to mention of The Kitchen.

Dane would take them by the spot the dolphins liked to play at this time of day. No Ibis Island native got tired of seeing them. Then, he would take them around the northern corner where the manatees hung out.

Liam stiffened. His eyes nearly popped out of his head. Dane turned to follow his gaze and saw Zoe and Harmony each holding beach towels to create a makeshift dressing room for Willow. Throwing his head back, Dane laughed and gave the engine some gas. He loved everything about Ibis Island, the Florida coast, and the water.

"Sun on your right, ladies and gentlemen. Pod on your left." This was a group of people who would understand his reference. The pod included about a half dozen adults plus two infants. They seemed to be having a day off, too, as they jumped high in the air in some kind of celebration.

They'd barely made it around the first bend when Dane smelled honeysuckle. It probably wasn't the safest way for him to drive a boat with seven passengers. Zoe handed him a mug. Iced tea.

"Peace offering," she said, wearing his favorite smile.

"I'll take it, but no peace offering necessary."

"I was curt."

"I get it." Then, he reconsidered. "No, actually, I don't. Maybe the staff doesn't care one way or another. Or maybe they'd be happy for us. They liked you when you were their boss."

"You can't understand."

She trailed her soft hand around his bicep, making him forget what they were talking about. He wanted to do this right, this he and Zoe thing. She'd gone along with his need to take their relationship slow. A few dinners like normal people. Walks on the beach. Only marginal taunting him with her lips or by pressing those damned perky C cups against him...like she was doing just then.

She turned his chin and kissed him with a quick peck as her last effort at an apology. If this is what he got, she should brush him off in front of his employees more often.

"Oh, my gosh!" Raine called from the front of the boat. "I can hear you smacking." She didn't bother lifting her head from her sun pose. "Gross," she added.

Harmony leaned on the rail, lifting her head to the sun. "You do need to get a room, kids. We could hold the beach towels for you."

He adored this family, Raine and all. "No manatees this morning. Sorry, Chloe." He was completely sincere. "We're coming up to the bird sanctuary. Which means we'll anchor with The Kitchen on port and the sandbar starboard." He turned up the tunes and slowed down.

When they anchored, Chloe pulled Liam in first. He helped her sift through the seaweed. Willow joined Raine who didn't move from her reclined spot in the front. Henry and Harmony took their time removing their t-shirts and wraps before gathering facemasks and snorkels.

"I'm hot," Zoe said and seemed to realize what she'd said just as it came out.

Dane smiled wide and placed his hands on her hips. She'd wrapped some sheer thing around her not-stick-figure hips and over her miniscule suit. He recognized it as the one she wore the day she found the skull.

"Let me rephrase." She tilted her head. "Let's get in the water."

"Please do," Raine called from the front.

He laughed over the music, picked up Zoe from behind her legs, toed off his shoes, and jumped in with her. Silky sand sifted between their toes. They circled and dove, slick limbs twining together. Her legs were smooth, her waist firm. He forgot his reason for taking it slow other than her entire family surrounded them. They stayed there longer then they should have, letting the tepid water cool the heat that built between them.

When stomachs began to grumble, Harmony made the men help with lunch as much as the girls. It was okay. He still adored her. They ate cucumber sandwiches on whole grain bread and something called Jicama Fries that Dane asked Harmony to refrain from explaining because they weren't half bad. The Kale Salad made his lips pucker and want a big, juicy steak, but all in all, it was a lunch he could get used to.

Dane leaned toward Liam. "You and Chloe brought in a haul."

"Twenty-six starfish and four seahorses. She made me put them all back. Here," he took out his phone. "Look at these." Liam showed him pictures of Chloe as if he were a proud dad. In the digital screen photos, Chloe's arms were each lined with careful rows of starfish.

He and Liam got *the look* from Harmony and put the phone away to help with clean up. Dane noticed Zoe check her phone, then move to the back of the boat to make a call.

There wasn't much clean up when the Clearwaters were involved. No gathering snorkels or masks. Everyone was conscientious of picking up after themselves. Out of habit only, he decided to make a quick inventory count before pulling the anchor. Ten masks, ten kick boards.

Zoe dropped her phone. She didn't reach to retrieve it and instead dangled her arms at her sides like they were dead weight. He got to her just before her legs gave out.

"Babe." He lowered her limp body to his lap on the nearest chair. "I've got you." Looking over his shoulder, all eyes were turned their way. Like a child, she curled into a ball on his lap, then covered her head with her arms.

No one crowded them. Even Chloe knew to be patient. They gave Zoe time, and so did he. He could feel drips of tears fall on the arm he used to hold her from sliding off his lap and onto the floor of the boat.

"It's okay," he whispered in her ear. "I'm here. We all are."

Her family lowered to the chairs that lined the perimeter of the boat.

There was only one thing that could bring this reaction from her. What kind of asshole gives this type of news to a woman over the phone? Cop or no cop, Osborne needed to have his ass kicked.

She rocked for a solid ten minutes as he rubbed her back. He kissed her forehead and realized he would easily give his right arm to take away her pain.

As if waking from a long night of sleep, Zoe lifted her head and looked around. She sat up, wiped her tears, and straightened the wrap that covered her legs. "It was Matt. He texted me and asked me to come see him." She shuddered once, hard, before going on. "I called him because I knew..." She cleared her throat. "I knew...He didn't want to..." The tears flowed freely down her cheeks like a steady winter rain. "It was him. It was Seth."

The sounds that came from Harmony were worse. There seemed to be nothing to compare to a mother's pain. Harmony may have been the rock, the glue of the family but she was a mother, and she was human.

They all suspected, maybe all intuitively knew it would be him, but this was what the grief of finality did to a family. The grief of death. The grief of murder.

FOURTEEN

Fresh flowers weren't Harmony's thing. Neither was a greeting card. Dane chose potted basil in a pot the shape of a manatee. He thought it might go well in her kitchen, but what the hell did he know about this crap? It had been days since he'd heard from Zoe. She was slipping away from him.

He waved at Henry who cared for the goats that lounged on the roof like nothing had changed. Harmony answered the door as he lifted his hand to knock. Her smile was serene. "This is three days in a row, dear. I'm keeping you from your work."

"I'm the boss." He smiled, but the words sent waves of sadness through him.

"Basil. How lovely. Come in, come in."

They sat in her sunny kitchen, and she did indeed place the manatee pot on the windowsill behind her sink.

Useless apologies for the scene on the boat had already been offered to him. Since there was no peeling Zoe from his arms, Liam had driven the boat back to Sun Trips. But where was she now? His arms were empty in more ways than one.

Willow came from the back room in her yoga gear. "Dane. Have you heard anything?"

He shook his head.

"Mom and I were just talking about when the three of us were children. Seth would try and flirt with girls. We got in his way."

"You didn't bother him, dear. He used you as bait. You were better than a puppy at the park when it came to attracting the girls."

They laughed an honest laugh. Dane needed to get a grip. This wasn't his family.

Willow sat in one of the polka dot painted wooden kitchen chairs and crossed her legs one over another.

"His fifth grade parent/teacher conference," Harmony said to Willow. "His teacher told me she had front door duty one morning when Henry dropped off Seth. Our ancient Corolla got to the front of the line and Seth climbed in the back seat, kissed Raine, then you, before getting out of the car. The teacher told me it made her cry."

This was a private moment. What was he doing here? Dane shook his head. "All I thought about as a kid was chasing skirts."

Harmony laughed, of all the damned things. "How do you think we had Seth? All Henry and I wanted to do was sneak whiskey from our parents' pantries and have sex on the beach."

"You kept him." It was a statement that was a question and profoundly inappropriate. By this point Dane wasn't sure if he had it in him to give a damn.

"It was our choice, yes." Harmony mimicked Willow and pulled up one of her legs. She took a deep breath as her mind wandered back thirty plus years. Then, she simply shrugged. "We wanted him. Our parents did everything they could to convince us otherwise, but we wanted him. Life as teenagers who just wanted to drink whiskey and have sex was certainly over, but it was our choice."

Harmony turned to him now, shoulders, face, and eyes. "Find her, Dane."

Willow kept her gaze down, but it didn't help. What the hell? "I don't know where she is." What would he say if he did find her? Where would he look?

"She's a woman, Dane. She loves you. Go find her."

And then, he knew. Butterflies burst in his gut. He knew where she would be. But what if he was wrong? What if the timing was off? He kissed Willow on the forehead, causing her to do a double take, before he did the same for Harmony. He ran out the door and waved backward at Henry as he jumped into his Jeep.

Zoe sat with her eyes closed and her legs crossed. She heard the quick rush of water between hundreds of fins as a school of fish darted in circles behind her. It mixed like a melody with the steady bubbles that released from her facemask. It was almost July and the water was warmer, so she chose her diving skins over her wet suit. A boat sped by too fast somewhere above. She tried not to focus on anything up there.

She wasn't putting herself at risk. Carefully, Zoe had used the charts and guidelines of underwater diving to ensure she wasn't coming down too often or too long. The last thing she wanted to do was to give herself decompression sickness and worry her parents any further.

He was with her here, Seth was. She could feel him. The memories were crisp. Ones of him carrying her on his shoulders when she was a little girl, all the way to the last dive they did together. It was here they dove last, not fifty yards away from where she found his skull. They'd spotted a grouper and took a zillion shots of it.

Sensing something was watching her, she opened her eyes but didn't move. Slowly, she glanced to the left, then right, keeping her breathing in controlled rhythm. It could be anything. Hiding in the seaweed. In a cavern. Behind a rock.

Of course something was watching her, she grinned. She was in the frigging Gulf.

Rotating, she started kicking lazily the fifty yards to the spot she found him. The water was choppy. Choppy was normal. The day she found him it had been unusually calm. Staring at the spot, she realized she would have never noticed the cavern under normal conditions. It was a mirage. No dark blue tint giving hint to the protruding opening.

She came to within five feet of it and waited. They had an agreement, her and the moray eel that made this its home. It poked its head out and tried to scare the hell out of her. Then, it bolted out of its hole, darting quickly in an effort to, once more, scare her before escaping the cavern and into the crevasse below.

Here, she'd found a skull with a knife through the eye. Her brother. Not much had been disturbed by the police. No yellow crime scene tape, she thought, sarcastically. Each of the last few days she'd come down here, she expected to find some sort of disturbance. Maybe rocks that had been chipped to release her brother from the wall. Or samples taken from around. Other than a small, jagged hole about the size of...of a knife, there was nothing.

She placed her hands on either side of the small opening, letting her legs dangle to the open water below. She felt something brush across her calf and assumed it was her friend. She would buy a new camera. A good one. Seth would want that. She would take out a loan and buy a Seth-approved camera and come down here to take pictures of her friend. He brushed her leg again. It made her smile, and she slowly inched herself from the crevasse. Friend or no friend, it was probably not a good idea to piss off a moray eel.

She came face-to-face with him. He wasn't an eel, and fear was nowhere to be found. Her body reacted regardless. Not with fear but an overwhelming warmth.

He came for her. The words repeated in her mind. He came for her. His beautiful, amazing blue eyes, although bloodshot, searched her face. She saw tenderness there and hoped she returned the same. If there was one thing she could have asked for at that moment, it would be to gaze into the eyes of Dane Corbin. He looked sad. She reached out and put her hand on his cheek. It was warmer than the warm water.

He took her air gauge and checked it. So Dane. Her eyes didn't leave his as he turned and read the instrument. It didn't make her want to slap him. Instead, she wanted to...she wanted him. Her insides erupted into a swirling hot tub of need. He came for her. He came for her, and he was crying. She tried to smile around her mouthpiece, trying to reassure him, but it didn't seem to soothe his expression.

He pointed up. She shook her head, took his hand, and tugged him toward the opening of Seth's cavern. He came for her. She needed to share this with him. In order to fit through the opening, their bodies pressed together from shoulders to knees. Even through their diving skins, the feel of his taught chest and thighs shot currents of desire throughout her. Taking his hand, she pressed his fingers along the small hole where the knife had been. He didn't flinch. He would do this for her.

His fingers moved along the inside of the wall and stopped on four slight divots she'd missed. They'd been smoothed over with the passage of time, giving the appearance of a soft pillow. How could anyone not appreciate underwater nature?

He pointed up again. This time, she nodded. He twined his

arms and legs around her, turning as they maneuvered out of the cavern. Remaining entangled, they began their ascent floating effortlessly together. The muscles in his legs flexed and released against her thighs as he slowly kicked his fins, moving them toward the light.

Halfway up, they made a decompression stop. Knowing the strength of his legs would be able to keep them at the proper depth, she wrapped hers around his waist, then pulled him to her. Who said water caused a man to shrink? He wanted her as much as she wanted him.

The careful arms that wrapped around her. The legs that continued to move against her backside. His obvious need for her. It was all killing her. She ached to rip her mouthpiece out and pour her lips over his. She pulled down the zipper of his wet suit and ran her hands over his abs, learning each square as they flexed in the water. Her fingers traveled up and over his chest, tracing a sailboat tattoo that covered his right pectoral.

Her breasts had not gone south since high school. She pressed them against him in an effort to prove it. Was he allowing her to break their take-it-slow pace? Because his hands slid around and took hold of her butt. He grabbed and kneaded, rhythmically pulling her against him. As their stop time ended, she pushed away, reading the expression in his eyes. They were no longer sad, but...determined.

Ten feet to the top. This was the longer stop that might possibly be her undoing. Glancing up, she didn't see the bottom of her boat. He'd led them to his.

She used the moment and ran the palm of her hand in a line from his throat, over his chest, then dipped into his suit. A large group of bubbles hurried from his facemask—his pupils dilating before returning to normal. It gave her the last bit of confidence she needed. She took his hand and placed it over her.

Quick and purposeful, his eyes left her face. He cupped her

from the outside of her suit as if she was lost treasure. Pulling her zipper, he traced his fingers along the swell of her flesh. His hands dipped beneath fabric, then tugged at her suit exposing her to the elements. Slick, cool water rushed over her. He circled with his thumbs as he explored, as the sound of the bubbles coming from their breathing apparatus quickened.

In the deep blue she saw something she'd dreamed about somewhere. *I can't quit thinking about you.* She could say the same, would say the same if they could get out of this damned water. Grabbing his wrist, she checked the gauge herself, then wanted to kick herself for taking his hand away from her. She wanted him, needed him.

Closing her eyes, she traveled her hand up and over his chest and rested both on his shoulders. Taking a slow breath, she forced herself to focus. He came for her. She would never forget it. They waited the last few seconds, before darting madly to the surface.

"Uh," she yelled as soon as her face hit the air. She yanked her mouthpiece away with one hand and his with the other, pressing her exposed chest to his and their lips together. Dane. Possessive. Hard. Needy. They turned in circles as their tongues did a dance that was a mix of reunion and awakening.

He rotated on his back, pulling her on top of him. "I found you," he crooned as he kicked his flippers toward the boat. "I'll never let you go again," he said between kisses. She thought her legs were helping, kicking as they closed the distance in the water, but she couldn't be sure. Her mind focused more on what was beneath her.

They tossed their gear onto his mini pier and pushed it randomly into the boat. She pulled herself up and collapsed on the floor. Turning over, she waited for him to follow, holding herself up with locked elbows and propped knees.

He came out of the water like a Greek god, his exposed chest and stomach muscles pumped from the dive. Water fell from his hair and wet suit as he stepped onto the boat, then let himself drop between her legs. The weight of him pressed into her core and covered her with everything she ever wanted.

The damned suits. Reading each other's thoughts, they unzipped and tugged, rolling the tight fabric free, then tossing the suits in a heap. She wrapped her legs around the back of him and pulled with her heels, throwing back her head and pressing heat to glorious heat.

His thick hands were everywhere, molding each inch of her. Cool lips traveled the length of her excruciatingly slowly. She wanted him more than anything she could remember. It had been too long, foreplay would have to wait.

Determined, she reached behind and unlatched the door to down below. It made him stop. He lifted his head in question. "Come," she said, and used sheer will power to push him off of her. Dripping down the stairs, she stumbled to the area that doubled as a living room and a kitchen nook. It was the only boat Sun Trips owned equipped with a bathroom and a bed. Had he chosen this one on purpose?

No.

This was her. Her want. Her need. Her resolution to take. She stood next to him with her bare toes over his. His chin nearly touched his chest as he looked down at her. He slid his hands up her waist, over the sides of her breasts, her shoulders until they rested, one on each cheek. His gaze was intense and moved from one of her eyes to the other. "You're mine." He kissed her, tenderly, lingering his lips on hers as he repeated. "Say you're mine."

It came out in a croak. "I'm yours." Two small words that made her legs buckle. He grabbed her backside with one hand, guiding her to the small couch. His other hand slowly pushed her until she was pressed against the back cushions. He sat back on his heels, seeming to study her. His eyes traveled over each part of her. Exposed, she felt the strongest desire to share everything with him. Reaching behind, she released the clasp on her top and ducked her shoulders out of it. His shoulders dipped forward as he exhaled in awe. His flattery gave her the nerve to do the same with the other half of her suit.

She watched as his deep inhale made the ship tattoo rise and fall. "You are the most beautiful thing in my world."

A tear escaped and slid down her cheek. She sat up and wrapped her legs around him as he kneeled. He wiped her tear with his thumb and followed it with his lips. Kissing her temple, her cheek. His fingertips led his lips on a slow path along the length of her collarbone, over the hollow at the base of her neck. One hand continued its trail south, but his lips didn't. They stopped and moved from one perky C to the other, assaulting her senses and leaving her a churning whirlpool.

He still had on his trunks. She wanted to rip them to shreds, but her arms wouldn't move, couldn't move. His lips on one side of her, his hand on the other, she could do nothing but let her head fall back and cry out.

When his fingers found her, her heels reflexively moved to the edge of the couch keeping her from breaking something. Her elbows locked as she grabbed his shoulders and cried out in celebrated release. Again and again, she shook as he took her to a place higher than any she knew existed. She could hear him coo her name as she kept going, coming down ever so slowly. In the midst of aftershocks, she found control of her arms and legs.

Desperately, she pulled his trunks, running her hands along his slick thighs, his muscled waist. His head dropped to her shoulder when she found him, hard as steel. He tried to slow her down, tried to bring her up again but she had waited too damned long for this.

"I don't have anything," she gasped. "Tell me you have——"
But he was already tearing open the package.

Guiding him, they came together in a meeting of bodies and
hearts. The sensation was more than she could have expected or
imagined. A moan came from him that made her heart melt
along with her body. She lifted, they moved. Faster and deeper,
pulling and grasping. He took her face, his brows dug so low, she
could barely see anything except the brilliant blue boring into
her. Her hands grabbed his sides, her nails dug in.

"Now." She didn't know if she said it out loud, but she
couldn't hold back another second. Her release was a desperate
panic to get closer, deeper. Without missing a beat, he clenched
her knees, readjusted her legs and dove in deeper. The muscles in
his sides flexed beneath her hands in his last push, holding them
there as his eyes turned opaque, then closed.

She was a limp noodle. The Coast Guard could be ordering
them out and she wouldn't be able to move her arms or legs. His
hair was still wet, but his skin no longer chilled. He pressed his
forehead to hers and squeezed his eyes shut. "You left me."

What? "What?"

"You left."

She had. Her shoulders were suddenly heavy. She left with
only a phone call to her mother, and escaped. He came for her,
and she took from him. How many times would he keep giving as
she kept pushing him away? "You're right. I was…No. I should
have called." She scooted over, so he could fit next to her, hoping
he would try.

He lay next to her, and she rested her head on his warm
shoulder. "You came for me." It made her lids sink. Please don't
let this be her final screw up.

"I know you needed——" he started.

"I should have——"

"——brought me with you."

"Would you have come?"

"I can't remember my life before you came crying to my office, asking me to buy Sun Trips."

She lifted her head to look into his beautiful blue eyes. "You mean that," she said as a statement.

He took her face in his hand. "You're mine," he repeated and guided her head back to his shoulder.

FIFTEEN

Zoe stood in the door of her parents' music room, the room that once was her brother's. She was in the middle of a line of Clearwaters. Her mother stood in front of her, her father just inside the room. Raine and Willow followed behind her. They'd been in this room a thousand times since Seth moved out at age eighteen and hundreds since his death.

This was profoundly different.

She let her mother take the time she needed. As strong as she may be, this was the first time she truly, truly accepted that Seth was gone. Not only gone, but brutally stolen from her.

In front of them lay the string and wind instruments that had been there for years. The empty space where Willow's old cello used to sit. And beyond these were two worn clothes dressers and a newer desk. Her parents had gotten rid of his kitchen table, chairs, couches, and bed. These three pieces were saved because Seth and their father had made them together.

"I don't want to do this," her mother seemed to say to the air.

Zoe placed a hand on her shoulder. "I know."

Her father interjected. "Seth kept secrets."

Zoe stood frozen as she took in the gravity of his words. "What do you mean, 'Seth kept secrets?' What kind of secrets?"

"We're not sure, dear," her mother answered for him. "He was a private person. We always respected that. I'm just not sure if his secrets are meant to be unearthed."

Bright light shone in through the window, making artificial ones irrelevant. She felt her mother's shoulder lift and fall beneath her hand.

"Secrets?" Raine butted in. "What the hell kind of secrets could Seth possibly have had?"

Walking as slowly as a bride down the aisle, her mother stepped to the first dresser. No clothing was left in these dressers. Inside were photo albums, shoe boxes filled with papers, and a few small trinkets Zoe remembered Seth had scattered around his apartment.

They brought back memories, crystal clear memories of where the items had been in his apartment or a story he might have shared about them.

It had killed Zoe to tell her mother about the break-in at Seth's old apartment building. She didn't want to turn it into a happy detail, but Zoe swore that each of her mother's windows were locked.

Her father went first. He took out a shoe box and handed it to Raine, then one for Willow, and a pile of envelopes for Zoe. Her mother reached in and took out a larger box of trinkets.

They sat on the floor in a circle and started thumbing through Seth's things, piece by piece. Subscriptions to treasure hunting magazines. Unpaid electric bills. The process should have been joyful reminiscing, but it wasn't. It was tedious and sad.

Her father pulled out something wrapped in a dishtowel. Everyone stopped to watch as he unwound the towel. Seth was a treasure hunter. Not like Dane. Dane would hunt anything, anywhere. Seth had eyes for only one treasure. Luciana Bezan's dowry.

It caused her mind to wander for a few moments. She couldn't remember the last time Dane went on a hunting trip, not even for a week. Was it last Christmas? No. He brought her mother a potted, table-sized Christmas tree, decorations included. It was the kind you plant after the holidays. It thrived at the edge of her parents' back yard at that very moment. It was one of the things she loved about D——

Did she love Dane Corbin? Her face tried to smile, but it wasn't the right time. When she looked up to see what her father had discovered, all eyes had moved to her. Her father held the something as it poked its seashell head out of the towel.

"What?" Zoe asked defensively.

Her mother grinned ever so slightly. "Never mind your sister, girls. Zoe finally got herself a roll in the hay."

"Mom!" Zoe complained.

Her sisters may be numb to her mother's antics, but her father should be spared the details of her love life. And how the hell did her mother know about her love life?

Raine made a face like she'd eaten a slice of lime. "Gross."

Henry ignored everyone and unwrapped the trinket. No priceless necklace. No silver tea cup or hand-made china. In it was the miniature sea-turtle sculpture their mother had made Seth for his thirtieth birthday out of tiny shells.

Tears fell down her mother's face. "He was such a good boy. I do hope he's happy wherever he is."

Her sisters took their boxes and stood. Relieved, Zoe did the same. They made some small talk about lunch on Sunday before Zoe went out to play Ultimate Frisbee, then took their assigned papers and left.

None of them were even close to the end of their mourning.

Zoe opened the front door of her home to find Dane standing with a duffle bag over his shoulder.

"You didn't look out the window before you opened the door."

"You have a bag."

"Partly because you don't look out the window before you open the door."

He was right. She really did need to get out of that habit. "Partly?" she asked and stood aside.

He walked past, sending his scent of leather and beach into her head and her heart.

"Why did I have to hear about the break-in at Seth's old place from your sister?"

Zoe assumed he meant Willow, not Raine. "I didn't have a chance to tell you." She'd been busy wallowing in her guilt for days. Then, had an afternoon…and night…of the best sex she'd ever had.

"We spent practically the entire day together yesterday."

"You're…distracting."

He smiled from ear to ear, making her knees weak. Slithering up to her and dipping his lips to her ear wasn't helping. They were warm and searching. Holy cow, the things he could do with his lips. Before she knew it, her hands were in his shirt. Was this real?

Her doorbell rang. Of course it was real.

She walked right over and opened it without looking out the window. She really didn't do it on purpose. He truly was distracting.

It was Raine.

"You have a key," Zoe said to her.

Raine walked in like she owned the place, much like Dane

had done. "Dane's Jeep is out there. I'm not taking that risk. Gross. Hello, Dane."

He nodded to her and headed into the kitchen.

"I'll be right back," Raine said and followed him in. This was going to be a long night.

The man she might possibly be in love with brought a bag with him to stay at her house. Her sister who's hated him since high school just followed him into her kitchen. The two of them were having a private conversation. Zoe plopped down on her couch and decided if she was going to have one of *those* nights, it would be a good time to go through some more of Seth's old mail.

She noticed an envelope from a travel agency. What if this was about the secret? Inside was a credit card receipt made out to United Airlines for $4,360. Where did he get that kind of money? And where was he going that cost that much to get to? It wasn't like him to even fly.

She flipped more and found a tax bill that would have never been paid. Stick it to the man, brother. Ad, ad, ad—then a business-sized envelope. She turned it over just as Dane and her sister came out of the kitchen.

"You look too happy," Zoe said as she unfolded the already opened end.

Dane sat next to her and set his feet on her coffee table, crossing them at the ankles. "We've come to an understanding."

After all this time they've come to an understanding? Her suspicious eyes turned to the paper she'd taken out of the envelope.

Raine sat in the loveseat and folded her arms. "When someone saves my baby sister once from a near drowning and again from herself," Raine shrugged. "I let bygones be bygones."

But Zoe was only half listening. She was busy reading.

"Only a short ten years later," he said as they spoke through her.

She flipped the envelope over, making sure she hadn't missed a name or an address somewhere.

When the two of them quieted, she read aloud.

'Dear Seth, I don't think I can get away. He's suspicious. He's always suspicious. I want to, but I'm scared. Tonight he told me he was going to put me away for good. I don't know what he meant, but I'm scared. I love you. I thought my life was nothing. Over. Then, there was you. Thank you for being you.'

No signature.

She looked up to her sister, then turned to Dane. "Seth had a mistress?"

"We should tell the cop," Raine barked.

It didn't set right with Zoe. "What? No. Why?"

"It's part of the puzzle. It's his job to judge, not ours."

"He wanted to take her away. Seth did. Do you think he loved her? We can't rat out someone he loved."

She watched as Raine inhaled deeply, then exhaled, letting her cheeks expand. "Point taken."

It was a relief to see Raine give in so easily.

"I wonder who she was...or is," Raine added.

Her pondering made all three of them sit back in consideration.

The sun beat down on Zoe's neck. She wished she had her cowboy hat, but Ultimate Frisbee with a cowboy hat wasn't a good mix. It was a busy Sunday afternoon in the central section of Ibis Beach, but beach goers were easy people. Everyone watched out for one another and rarely did anyone mind an occasional Frisbee on their blanket. A consistent wind blew from the Gulf. The scattered white, fluffy clouds provided sporadic reprieve from the ruthless sun.

The sand sifted between her toes as Zoe backed up, judging the angle of the Frisbee, deciding where it would come down. She'd been right weeks before. Dane subbed for her one time and was good enough to earn an open invitation. Lucky for her, he was on her team.

Always keeping up his Sun Trips image, he wore his baggy shorts and leather bracelets. They played shirts and skins. Lucky for their entire team, they were the skins. The girls on both sides could hardly concentrate on the game. His muscles flexed beneath the barbed wire on his left bicep. They were able to get a rare glimpse of the ship on his pectoral.

It was funny how differently she saw him now. He didn't carry himself like someone who always had a dozen sets of female eyes trained on him.

'You're mine.' The memory of his words sent a splash of energy through her just as she jumped to catch the throw-off toss. The other four members of her team darted around, dodging opponents and signaling when they felt they were open. Flicking her wrist, she sailed the Frisbee in a beeline to the new girl who caught it, froze her feet as the rules required, but then tossed it right into the hands of the other team.

The interceptor was too excited with foiling Zoe's toss and took a step with the Frisbee. Error. Time out was called as the Frisbee changed hands, stopping the game where they stood.

"Lookin' sah-weet, Zoe," said the only other guy on their side. "Your throwing as good as your digging up skeletons?"

Her eyes went to Dane. She wasn't sure why. He stood with his water bottle analyzing her. He didn't approach. Half the players worked for Sun Trips. She had a hard enough time keeping them from thinking she sold Dane her business so he would sleep with her. She appreciated his understanding as he kept his distance.

The comment didn't unsettle her as much as Dane might have thought. It was harmless. The guy couldn't know how deep it cut. It made her take a look around. People were everywhere. Some watching them. Some not. Someone on the island knew the 'skeleton' she found was Seth. But who?

Dane made his way over to her. His attempt to appear casual wasn't so convincing. He lifted his arm in the telltale signal of a 360 high five. She didn't leave him hanging and copied his movements, passed the high five, then slapped their hands between their hips. She caught the scent of leather and sand.

A round of jumping chest bumps between the guys and high-fives between the girls finished the time out, and Zoe whizzed the Frisbee to Dane from the sidelines.

Dane tossed it to the new girl, giving her a chance to redeem herself? She caught it as he ran into the end zone. He might have been able to score if she threw it to him, but the man who covered Dane was good, really good. Dane dodged and faked but never gave the signal he was ready for a pass. The new girl flicked it to Zoe who was able to nearly keep the Frisbee in motion as she continued the pass onto the man open on the other side of the end zone. Point.

It was time for a well-earned water and gloating break. The new girl jumped on Zoe's back, cheering her assist.

Zoe's brows dug deep, she turned her head one way, then the other. Why hadn't she realized it? After all this time, she hadn't realized the person who attacked her at her parents' home wasn't a man. Wasn't a small man, but a woman.

SIXTEEN

"This doesn't feel right." Zoe sat in the passenger seat of Dane's Jeep, driving up 275. She'd convinced him to give it a day. Sleeping on a big decision was always smarter. Almost always.

He didn't respond with words but laced their fingers together and traced circles around the inside of her wrist with his thumb. He hadn't even let her finish her sentence when she tried to talk him into waiting longer to report Seth's affair. And the fact that she remembered her attacker was female. Maybe Dane was right. Sleeping on it didn't change anything. Seth was having an affair, and it was a woman who broke into her parents' home...also probably her house and Seth's old apartment, too. Coincidence? This was a necessary tattle.

Calm waters lay to either side of her, like they were the day she found Seth's remains. She wanted to be down there, with him. But he wasn't there. Just her friend, the moray eel.

She still needed to tell her parents and her sisters the attacker was female. A strong female. Or was Zoe a wimp who frightened more easily than a trapped mouse?

She couldn't imagine what it would be like to be abused or feel afraid to leave someone. Then again, anyone who could break into someone's house could be capable of lying their butt off. Raine was right, they would let Matt do the judging.

Dane parked in new car parking. Why was that suddenly cute?

He walked to her and wrapped his arm around her waist. It was one those things that was starting to be blessedly natural. The look on his face puzzled her but for whatever reason didn't make her inquire. His smile was content; it was complacent. He reached down and kissed her on the top of her head before continuing on. A wave of warmth rolled throughout her before landing in the center of her heart.

The receptionist had been told to send her up. He was waiting when they exited the elevator. Matt and Dane extended hands at the same time.

"Good to see you, Dane. How have you been?"

"Good and bad, as I bet you can imagine. Zoe's got something for you."

Matt's eyes turned to her, and she nodded. They stepped into Matt's office and she took her usual chair. Zoe noticed a white box with some letters and numbers written above the word 'Clearwater.'

Seth's skull might be in there. And the knife. A sheet of clammy sweat erupted over her skin. Her body language had always given her away in everything she did. Her blushing was only the beginning. They both must have been able to read her, because Matt grabbed the box and took it somewhere out of his office as Dane turned to her.

"He didn't mean it," he whispered and took her hand in his.

She must look bad if he was sticking up for Matt. "I know. Of course, I know. Seth isn't in the box." She tried to sound like her mother, but she wasn't.

"Well," Matt said as he came back in his office. "Now that I've been an ass, what can I do for you?"

She tried to laugh, but it came out as a sickly squeal. Straightening in her chair, she worked at appearing professional. This was a case, right? A detective's case.

A case that might draw the line between making or breaking her. So, no pressure there.

She took a deep breath and dove in, relinquishing the letter to him. It was postmarked at the Ibis Island Post Office a few days before Seth's…murder. Then, she explained her epiphany that the person who attacked her was female.

Matt scratched his chin. "And you say you found the letter before you decided your attacker was female?"

She knew where he was going with this and didn't like it. "No. A girl on my Ultimate Frisbee team jumped on my back and made me remember I had breasts shoved in my back the night my parents' home was broken into." It sounded worse after she tried to explain. How did she miss that before? Dammit. Now, he had her second-guessing herself. "I would have never thought a woman could do that. I assumed it had to be a man until the gal jumped on me. It made me remember." Yes. Digging herself a hole.

"Could be, Zoe. Definitely. We're bringing in the other men who were in the group Seth dove with the day of his death."

The group that each had a diving partner except Seth. She shook her head, keeping herself from going down that road.

"They did that already, two years ago," Dane interrupted.

"New evidence. New questioning. Can't hurt."

Matt's tone was condescending, and she didn't like it. "What did you find out about the evidence?" she asked as Matt looked over the letter for himself.

"I assume you're speaking of the murder weapon, and we're not going public with that yet."

142

"I'm not public," she protested.

He looked at her with cop eyes. "I'm afraid I can't give you any information that might compromise your brother's case."

She felt like Raine and wished her sister were here to set him straight.

"You're smart enough to know I can't share confidential information about a pending investigation. Do you want me to mistrial your brother's case before we make it to trial?"

"Make it to trial? Do you have a suspect? Who is it?" She nearly jumped out of her seat.

"No, no. Now, take a breather there."

She could slap him.

"One step at a time. I'll keep you updated on everything I can. I won't forget. This is good." He waved the letter. "It could be a motive. I'm glad you brought it."

A motive? As in someone killed her brother because someone found out Seth was having an affair?

"Well, I can tell you right now," she thought out loud. "Richard Beckett is gay. His partner is definitely not a woman. And—"

Matt held up a finger as he opened a file from the side of his desk and started thumbing through. It was Seth's file. She wanted to read it so badly she could taste it.

"The realtor," he said knowingly.

"Yes," she answered curtly. "The realtor. Why isn't this, *I share, then you share?*"

He lifted his eyes to her as Dane injected, "This isn't a game, Zoe. This is murder." There he was again. Sticking up for the cop. Where was Raine when she needed her?

"Timothy Hart," she offered reluctantly. "School Superintendent. He never married. The letter refers to a husband."

Matt nodded and took notes.

"The rest are up for grabs. The police chief and Blake

Eaton...he's the Show Me's owner...both fit the asshole status, but abuse? I don't know. Wait a minute. Blake Eaton's wife is younger than me. I can't see Seth with someone barely old enough to drink legally." She started imagining the other wives with Seth.

"It might not have been someone in his diving group," Matt suggested. "Try to keep an open mind."

Wow. She hadn't even considered it. He was right. Each diver had the same story the days after Seth's disappearance. They just felt awful about it. One minute Seth was there, the next he wasn't. The last time they'd spotted him was at the mouth of the larger crystal springs cavern.

She'd found three more letters. After Matt's refusal with transparency, she was reluctant to turn them over to him. Yet. Her family never saw the first one. Maybe she would share these with them before she gave them to Matt. Maybe she would make copies of each. Maybe she would just keep them to herself. First, she would read them each a dozen more times.

'My dearest Seth, I'm so sorry for my reaction when you mentioned having kids. Of course I want to have children with you. The thought of cuddling on a porch swing with you and our son or daughter is a dream I'll keep forever. I'm just not sure I can have children after...after. I love you. Maybe we can adopt. I love you...'

He wanted children with this woman? Zoe rubbed her face over her hands. How did he keep such secrets from all of them?

Her life was becoming more and more surreal. Dane was spending his sixth night at her place. It was as natural as breathing now. They were sitting on her couch, Zoe with her legs over his lap. He used them as a desktop for his Sun Trips bookwork.

She wasn't sure if she felt guilty because he was doing the bookwork that used to be hers or because he was staying at her place due to the recent break-ins. "You don't have to stay, you know."

He didn't answer with words. It was more of a grunt as he kept his eyes on his paperwork. It felt like a challenge. Pulling her legs from his lap, she destroyed his lumpy, make-shift table top. Crawling the short distance between them, she straddled him as he dropped his papers next to them.

"You're…um…happy to see me." Very happy.

He didn't laugh at her attempt at humor. Instead, he slid his hands up her blouse sending her from zero to sixty in seconds. His hands. She let her head fall backward. His glorious, magical hands. How did she ever live without them?

She shifted just enough to make him suck in a quick gulp of air. Dane Corbin could multi-task. He soothed and caressed, teased and molded. Dipping his fingers beneath her lace, he tugged enough to cause her to lift her head. She needed to see his blue eyes, see them as they turned a shade deeper.

Her damned, damned, flipping cell rang. It was Raine's ring-tone. She looked at the time. Eleven-thirty. "I'd better get it."

This time his growl was much sexier.

"Can you get out?" Raine asked. "I'm at the north end of the island with a disorientation. I just got a call about a rental with the porch lights on in front of an early nest that's near its hatching due date."

"Are you sure you want me?" Zoe asked. "Shouldn't you call Willow?"

"Nah. You don't need a permit to knock on a patio door. Unless you're chicken."

She was not. "Give me the address, smart ass. Oh, and I found some more letters. I'll let you see them before I hand them over to Matt this time."

"More letters? Really. And thanks. You should've known Osborne wouldn't return the first one. A pig's a pig."

She slung a leg over Dane like she was dismounting. "I've gotta check out a patio light left on beach side. You don't need to come with. Get your bookwork done."

"Like hell."

SEVENTEEN

The only sounds on the beach at this hour were the waves as they crashed. Since it was dark, Dane opted to keep his sandals on. Zoe had, too. They were the only ones strolling the beach for nearly as far as he could see. Much farther south the telltale signs of two flashlights bobbed along the beach. Probably tourists.

Flashlights weren't really necessary. The sand was a light tan, almost white. It reflected off the distant crescent moon and lit their path. Still, they carried turtle friendly flashlights just in case. Covering the bulb with amber colored cellophane didn't take much time. He thought the realtors should provide the covers in all their rentals.

As they came closer, the lights from the patio in question were like a lighthouse showing him and Zoe the way. Unfortunately, it would do the same for sea turtle hatchlings if they decided to emerge that night.

"Where is the nest?" he wondered aloud.

She pointed inland as they walked. Four wooden stakes stood guard around the nest with bright, orange tape wrapped around them. It looked like a mini crime scene. The number for Ibis Island Turtle Conservation was in black magic marker on the stake in the front. Raine's cell.

He stopped at the nest and studied it more carefully. No movement that he could see. "Which numbers tell when the eggs were laid?"

"We don't put that information on the stakes anymore. People were starting to figure out when the nests were due to hatch and disrupted the hatchlings. The numbers tell which section and the chronological order the nest was made within this section. See? Section 3. This is Oliver's section. And the 2 is because this was the second nest laid in his section."

"You're sexy when you're businesslike." It was true. He took her free hand as they continued, reaching the path that led to the rental.

"Damn it." She set her clipboard and flashlight down and picked up a lounging chair. "Raine didn't say, but I'm going to go out on a limb and assume this is one of Beckett's rentals. He's notorious for leaving chairs out." She walked to the rental's beach entrance and stacked the chair on top of the one furthest from the shore.

There were at least a dozen of them lined up neatly parallel to the beach. She reached for the next chair when one in the middle moved. He stuck out his arm, stopping her. "That one moved."

"What moved?"

"The chair."

She pushed his arm away. "Chairs don't move."

Before she could argue that he was seeing things, it moved again.

"Richard frigging Beckett. This is exactly why we ask each and every one of the realtors to stack their chairs." She walked closer, dipping her head underneath.

It was a turtle. A huge, gorgeous loggerhead. Stuck under the chair.

Zoe tugged at the chair. It wasn't budging. The turtle was slow on the sand but still tried to get away from Zoe and the chair. "She could have dragged this all the way out to the water. Damned Beckett. She would drown."

"Let me give it a try." It was stuck all right. And the turtle was heavy as hell. He tried to slide it off the way it would have ducked into it. That seemed to be working, but the turtle kept inching back underneath it. Dane headed around, stepping on some sea oats as he tried to get in front of it.

"Hey. Those are protected plants."

He didn't give her the luxury of a glance. "Sea oats or turtle? Make a choice."

Her silence would serve as his answer.

He slipped it off, freeing her, only to have her head inland.

"We've got her freaked out," Zoe said.

"How much did you say these things weigh?"

"Three hundred pounds, minimum. You can't pick her up. You're not certified."

"Hell," he said as he reached for the sides of her shell.

"No, behind the back of her head and above her tail."

"I thought you didn't know how to do this." His head nearly exploded when he lifted. Using his thighs as a fulcrum, he pivoted the beast toward the shore. Her flippers waved like mad making it all the harder not to drop her. Nearly plopping her in the sand, she spotted the water and started her trek down the beach. It looked like she was swimming free style over the sand. It was…frigging amazing. As soon as she hit the water, her stroke turned to butterfly with both flippers pulling up and around her before smacking the water and propelling her forward. He stood motionless and watched the water long after she was gone. To free a helpless creature was magnificent as it was, but add that it was an endangered helpless creature…it was something he would never forget.

He felt a nudge. Oh, right.

The rental was the type you'd expect to see on an island off the coast of Florida. Bright coral paint, rows of shells plastered in the stucco walls. He stopped short when they hit the back of the patio. In the brick were plastic toys in the shapes of necklaces, hunting knives, and china. Written in chips of colored rock, the edge of the patio read, "Luciana's Dowry." He wasn't sure why, but it unsettled him enough to take her arm and step in front of her.

He led the way to the back door. The blinds were open, letting out extra light toward the beach. Inside were two men and two women sitting around a table playing cards and drinking wine. It was a good thing they were awake. Tourists might not like having someone knock on their door at this hour. He didn't blame them. It could be their first time on the island, or maybe they came regularly, as many do. They might not know to turn off their patio light. Not if the rental owner didn't include it in the contract or post it in the rental.

Luckily, Zoe had remembered her Island Turtle Patrol shirt. She knocked and the voices stopped. All heads turned their way. He imagined they were deciding what to do. She knocked again.

A woman answered. She looked to be in her forties or fifties. Another woman and two men stood behind her. That's right. Have the woman open the door.

"Hello," Zoe greeted them. "We're from Ibis Island Sea Turtle Conservation. We're sorry to bother you at this time of night, but we need to ask you to turn off your patio light. We have turtle nests close by and—"

"Oh, we're sorry. Does the light hurt them? Are they coming out right now?" The woman craned her head around Zoe. It's what most tourists came to the island for. The turtles.

"The light can confuse them, yes," Zoe explained. "We don't have any hatching at this moment, but some of the nests close by are due soon. If you could just turn off your lights on this side of the house at dusk, we would appreciate it. So would the turtles."

The woman reached over and flicked the light. "We came three years ago and got to see one crawl up on the beach."

"Oh, how lovely." Zoe never turned away from an interested tourist. "Did she lay eggs for you?"

"No." The woman looked positively crushed. "It was one of those pretend…"

"False crawls?" Zoe amended.

"Yeah. One of those. Maybe this year."

"Maybe. Good luck, and remember to leave your flashlights off if you walk the beach at night. I hope you see one."

He linked fingers with her as they made their way back to his Jeep. Experimenting, he ran his fingertips down the inside of her arm. She shivered. Her erogenous zones were exceptionally sensitive. The more he learned, the more there was to know, and the more he wanted to learn.

She was becoming an addiction. It left him out of his element. But that was what he was trying to resolve, wasn't it? Was he going to spend the rest of his life in flip-flops on a boat hunting for treasure? Lucky had tried to get him back out on the ocean. There was a time when he wouldn't have wanted anything else. Why did he have no desire to take Lucky up on the offer?

Zoe.

"You're quiet," she said in the almost alto croon that kept him awake at night.

It was worse than getting caught having a sex fantasy.

"Who do you think Seth was having an affair with?" she asked.

It was like a necessary cold shower.

"Do you think it was the wife of one of the divers?"

151

"Osborne said anyone could have been down there."

They turned down the long, skinny beach access trail that led to his Jeep.

She stopped and pulled on his hand.

"Forget something?" he asked.

She fidgeted for a full minute before muttering, "I'm falling in love with you." Her eyes shone up at him like emeralds hiding in a damned shipwreck.

"It's the picking up the turtle and the way you wait for me when I come in from a tour. And those damned bracelets and the wrinkles that form between your eyes when you do Sun Trips bookwork. And the Smithsonian. I think I started to fall when I found out about the Smithsonian."

When had she found out about the Smithsonian? Her gaze dropped to her feet.

He used a finger to lift her beautiful chin. She trembled beneath his finger. A single tear slipped between her closed lids, then another. He pressed his lips to one of her eyes. "And I'm in love with you." Then, kissed the other. "I think I've been since the day you came crying in my office, asking me to buy you out."

She opened her eyes to him. The green turned bright beneath the salt from her tears. "But I'm just me."

He shook his head and kissed her on the lips this time. "You have no idea who you are, Zoe Clearwater."

"I can't believe we're doing this," Dane said to Zoe for the third time.

He was right, of course, but she couldn't just sit around waiting, and Matt wasn't sharing. She'd convinced Dane to take her Jeep. His was an ostentatious beacon. He drew the line at letting her drive. She didn't have the energy to argue about the chauvinistic push. Opening her glove box, she pulled out the pad of paper she'd started taking with her everywhere she went.

They sat outside Blake Eaton's home. It was beachfront and looked like a log cabin. She thought it seemed like it belonged in a forest, not on an island off the coast of Florida. They hoped to get a glimpse of his new wife, or better yet to follow her if she left.

As a person who never left the island—hardly ever—she was the one up to date on island gossip. "I've never met his new wife," she explained. "He divorced his former wife five years ago. Traded her in for a younger version. Do woman-abusers divorce their wives? I thought they kept them. Possessive and all that."

"No offense, but I'm not sure a woman who was raised by Henry and Harmony Clearwater is qualified to know about life in an abused home."

"Hmm. Good point," she had to agree.

"What are we looking for?" he asked.

"I don't know. To see what the new wife is like? I can't really see Seth with a woman younger than me." Her nose curled at the idea.

"I'm not sure either of us would know what an abused woman looks like," he said.

A brush of conflict flowed into her. Zoe's attacker was possibly abused. Severely. She wanted to hate her, but...Dane was right. She had no clue what abuse could do to a person. She flipped through her notes as they sat. "Timothy Hart. Superintendent to all Ibis Island schools. Never married, but that doesn't mean he doesn't have a woman."

"The letters said, 'husband.'"

That's right. She was no good at this.

"Glen Oberweiss' wife is about the right age, if there is a right age. She seems like a nice person. See? That's where I get mixed up. I'm trying to find someone nice enough Seth would fall in love with her. Except she's also the kind who breaks into people's homes and attacks…well…me."

"Just the facts, then. Who has a wife?"

"Oh jeez, there she is," Zoe sunk in her seat. It wasn't like they were the only car parked along the street. Several people had already left their cars to use the handy beach access near the Eaton's home.

The woman came strutting out in cork wedges, shorts, a tank, and big, perfect hair.

"No big sunglasses hiding a black eye," Dane commented.

"Yeah," she added. "I can't picture Seth with her. Or her trying to choke me or anyone else. She might break a nail."

EIGHTEEN

Z oe lay still and mentally sorted what she'd discovered.
Whenever she had time off, she staked out the homes of the men who were there the day Seth was murdered. She took pictures with Dane's camera. It was one Seth would approve of. Dane came with her every time, reminding her he was the boss and set his own hours. The elbow jabs, looks, and eye rolls from the other employees increased exponentially from the obvious way they often left at the same time.

Since the public school superintendent wasn't married, and the realtor wasn't married to a woman, they focused on the other four that were in Seth's diving group the day he was murdered.

They doubted Seth's involvement with Blake Eaton's beach bunny, trophy wife, but the mayor's wife could be a possibility. As well as the police chief's and the town historian's wife. Pictures of each were taped to the pad of paper Zoe had deemed *the investigation notebook*. She thumbed through it as Dane breathed deeply next to her.

The sun wasn't up yet. Her beach walks three days a week made it difficult to sleep in on the other four days. Luckily, the moon shone through the blinds enough for her to read her notes without turning the light on. She was going to buy a book light the next time they hit the store.

They.

The knee-jerk internal reference made her set her pad of paper on her chest and turn her head toward him. Dane Corbin was in her bed. And had been every night for weeks. They were in love. When had her life turned upside down?

He slept splayed with one of his legs draped over hers. It kept her grounded and warm both metaphorically and literally. His arm sprawled around her head, with his hand resting on her opposite shoulder. She used his tattooed bicep as a pillow.

When they were together, she never thought about the locks on her windows. Or felt the woman as she attacked from behind, then pushed her into Willow's old cello.

His eyelids fluttered twice, then opened. The first thing she noticed was the striking blue as it practically glowed in the dark. He was searching for her. She smiled as he found her, then focused his beautiful sleepy eyes. His hair was a disaster and adorable bags sat beneath his eyes telling them both it was too early to be awake.

"You're an early riser," he croaked.

"Did I wake you?"

He shook his head and pulled her into him. Resting her head on his chest, his sail boat tattoo stabbed holes into her heart. He was long overdue for a trip. She wasn't that kind of woman, was she? The kind who tried to keep her man chained to her? He should be out on a boat with Lucky Nemo if that's what he wanted.

She propped herself on her elbow and looked down at him. "When are you heading out for your next treasure hunt? I've seen the maps and journals you leave up on your computer." She sounded like a stalker. "Not that I'm reading your stuff. I'm not. I just think you should get out. Did you and Lucky make a plan when he was here?" She was rambling a mile a minute at 5 a.m. when he'd barely gotten a chance to fully open his eyes. He had every right to bolt out the door and never come back.

Instead, he looked up at the ceiling and wrapped his arms around her tighter. Kissing the top of her head, he answered her battery of questions. "I don't have plans for another trip. The maps and journals I'm looking at are about Luciana's Dowry. I'm curious. And I'm not leaving you until this is settled."

He was leaving her after 'this is settled?' She was reading too much into his statement. Worse yet, she knew she was but couldn't help it.

"I'm going to track Mrs. Green this morning."

"The mayor's wife?"

"Yes. The pictures we have of her are from far away. I'm going to go and see if she leaves anywhere on her Tuesday mornings. Maybe I can catch her at the store or at one of the coffee shops. Then, I'm going to visit my mother, and then I'm going to corner Matt. We have information he could use...sort of. He needs to reciprocate."

He kissed her ear lobe, then trailed his hands down and cupped her backside. Holy sea turtles. Treasure hunt what? Mrs. Green who? She smiled into his chest. "Are you sure you don't want more sleep?"

He pulled her completely on top of him.

Oh. "I guess you're sure."

The goats had already been led up the winding path to the roof for the day. Dew dripped down the leaves of the palm tree that stood in the corner of her parents' front yard. Zoe parked in the street, then looked up to the sky. Not a cloud in sight, but that could be deceiving. An Ibis Island storm could erupt from a cloudless sky in minutes. She'd checked the weather app on her phone when she was staking out Mrs. Green's home like some sort of PI. A PI or a criminal. No rain in sight for this PI/criminal. So, she left the soft top of her Jeep down.

Zoe decided her morning thus far was a success. She was able to—possibly criminally—follow Mrs. Green to the bank. Mrs. Green didn't give Zoe a look like she was the person she'd attacked during a break-in. Although they ran in different circles and different socio-economic statuses, Mrs. Green seemed to be a lovely woman. Confident, beautiful, polite.

Zoe picked some lemon balm leaves from the pot on the front porch on her way into her parents' house. "Hello," she called as she entered.

"Back here, dear." It was her mother's voice.

She found her parents sitting in the four seasons room they added to the back of the house when Zoe was in second grade. Glass on three sides, her mother sat in beams of sunlight reading a book with her legs propped on Zoe's father's lap. It reminded Zoe of sitting in her living room with Dane.

"No Dane?" her father asked. Speak of the devil.

Zoe plopped down on the window seat across from them. "He lets me out alone in broad daylight, if I'm in a public place...or if I want to visit my parents."

Without moving her eyes from her book, Zoe's mother added, "I always knew he was a good boy."

It made Zoe's brows drop. "You did, didn't you?"

"It's easy to see what's in a person's heart."

No it wasn't, Zoe thought, as her father took her mother's hand in his. It was an unconscious movement. A physical connection between two people who loved each other. It was beyond Zoe's mental peripheral vision to imagine sitting like that with Dane thirty-some odd years from now.

"You fit well together. The way you move around each other is like a dance between two people in love. Oh, you brought in lemon balm leaves." Her mother tossed her legs from Zoe's father as quick as a schoolgirl. "I'll heat some water."

As she headed to the kitchen, her mother added, "Detective Osborne called. He wants me to have a funeral."

What? "That's none of his business." Zoe tried not to sound as irritated as she was. She was definitely beginning to look at Matt as Raine looked at all police officers.

"That's what I said, dear. They won't even give us Seth's remains, and they want us to have a funeral. I told him we were planning on spreading what little ashes we'll have over the Gulf during an intimate celebration of life."

"He thinks it will fish out Seth's mistress," Zoe said as a statement. She didn't want to admit it, but it was a good idea.

———

Zoe approached the Sun Trips pier with a pontoon loaded full of snorkeling/eco tour passengers. They had their beach bags over their shoulders and their sand dollars in their hands. The word that came to mind was Matt's, 'lame.' She missed taking out scuba groups. Consequences.

To make matters worse, Dane wouldn't be waiting for her when she docked. He and Liam were out with a not-lame group of six customers completing the last portion of their scuba diving certification requirements. She missed it like she'd lost a best friend.

A man stood by the picnic table in the shelter created for customers who waited for a boat tour. As she approached, she made out the dress pants and gun holster. Matt.

She trolled close to the pier, assuming he would tie up the pontoon for her. Then, she remembered he was from Chicago.

"Thank you for using Sun Trips Touring, ladies and gentlemen," she said as she hopped out and tied the boat herself. "I hope you enjoyed your ride. We have bathrooms just inside the doors and to the right."

"Hello, Matt." She suspected why he was here. "I'll be just a minute."

"Can I give you a hand?" Now, he asks. She smiled at his naivety. "I've got it, thanks."

He backed off and sat on the picnic table while Zoe prepared the boat for the evening party tour. He was here about the funeral, she assumed. He was going to try and get her to convince her mother to hold a funeral.

After turning in the tips jar, she chose a spot across the table from him and slung her legs over the long seat. "What can I do for you?" she asked honestly.

"Is there somewhere we can talk?"

She looked around. No one was within earshot. "Here's as good as any. What's up?"

He let out a heavy sigh. "You've been staking out suspects."

Well. She didn't see that one coming. Tilting her head, she considered. "The only way you would know that is if you were staking them out, too."

"Not me personally."

"Same difference."

He sighed. "So…did you learn anything?"

"Oh no, you don't. This time it's you share, I share." She folded her hands and placed them on the table for added emphasis.

"This is a murder investigation, Zoe."

"That's right. The murder of my brother."

Another heavy sigh. "The murder weapon was an antique knife."

Her brows lifted. She never actually expected him to cave. And so quickly.

"What does that mean?"

"It leads to some possibilities."

"Like?"

"Your turn."

Ah. "I can't see Seth with Blake Eaton's wife. She's too young and too blonde, if you know what I mean."

He nodded.

"We've already discounted Richard Beckett, the realtor, and Timothy Hart, the school superintendent. That leaves the mayor's wife, Mrs. Green, the town historian's wife, Mrs. Oberweiss and Chief Robert's wife. Mrs. Green is very nice, but I'm not sure, and I haven't gotten a close up of Mrs. Oberweiss or Mrs. Roberts."

"Good to know."

"Your turn," she reminded him.

"If you're going to plan a murder, the best murder weapon… if you're a murderer…is a common knife, like a steak knife from a large restaurant chain. The fact that the knife was unique leads me to believe the murder wasn't planned."

"Have you identified the knife?"

"No. I've combed through historical journals and books and can't find a match. I've found some that are close. It seems to be from the 18th century." He paused and stared at her. "I'd like for your family to hold a public funeral for your brother."

There it was. "We're Clearwaters. A private celebration of life, maybe. A public funeral?" She shook her head.

"I need to try and flush out the mistress."

It was her turn to sigh heavily. She looked out over the water. Choppy and shadowed with cloud cover. "You really think it would help?"

"I do, yes."

"I might be able to convince my mother it would help solve the case."

He looked around as if someone may have suddenly came within earshot. "I tried that tactic."

"You're not a woman."

"Thankfully this is true. I want that funeral. I'm trusting you, because I need you. And because this is about your brother." He took her hand. It wasn't sensual. He was a friend. A good friend.

Hoots and hollers came from the water. They turned their heads to a boat full of newly certified scuba divers as it approached the pier. Liam maneuvered the ski boat behind the pontoon as Dane signed papers. Four men and two women. All over forty, if she had to guess. They were positively beaming. She should be happy for them. But she wasn't. At that moment she was all about pity. Pity for her brother. Pity for the woman he left behind. Pity for her mother who would have to face a public circus held in honor of her son. And pity for herself and the life she'd left behind.

NINETEEN

Since her talk with Matt, Zoe felt a twinge of guilt anytime she brought out Seth's letters. It wasn't like she'd been keeping them from him. She gave him every original. She'd just made copies first. Okay, so she made copies for both of her sisters and her mother, too. It's not as if they would leave them out for any visitors to find. Or a passing by husband-abused woman who wanted to break into their house.

She took a rare moment to enjoy the beach. The spot at the south end of the island, just where the beach began to stretch east, was a quiet place with few people. Her toes dug into the soft, warm sand. She propped herself on her half beach chair with a cotton towel beneath her. Normally, she would read a book on these rare occasions. Today, she had letters. Letters and the Gulf.

'My dearest Seth: Let's do it. I'm ready. I'm scared as can be and just as excited. Are the tickets for somewhere far away? No, don't tell me. It's best if I don't know. Are you sure you're okay with this? About leaving your family? You love them, but he's too powerful. His connections…If we tell anyone where we're going, we'll put them in danger. And you know how smart he is when he's not drinking.'

He drank. Zoe made a mental note of it. Seth loved this woman, didn't he? It made Zoe incredibly sad he hadn't told her. Both because he didn't trust her and because they were too scared to share.

A small group of Ibis birds waded in the bubbly waves with their tall legs and long beaks, feeding in the water. Here, she didn't need to remind small children not to run and scatter the birds. Each bird on the island needed every opportunity they could to fatten up on natural foods for their subsequent migration or to regain the fat they'd lost from marathon sessions of sitting on their eggs. The last thing they needed was children chasing them away from dinner.

The funeral was late that afternoon. She kept thinking of it as an artificial show…a set up. But it wasn't. Seth deserved some kind of ending, and if this was going to be it, she would make the best of it.

The guest list was ridiculous. They invited everyone they could think of and placed an open invitation/announcement in the paper. Zoe tried to tell Matt it was too obvious, but he said Seth's mistress would show regardless. There were still things he wasn't telling her. She shrugged to herself. He was a cop. Just not the kind Raine thought he was.

She would go, smile, and search the eyes of each and every woman who came to offer her condolences and say good-bye to a lover. Zoe would also gain her own closure and say good-bye to him. A tear escaped over her lid. She took advantage of the alone time and let herself have a full-out cry. She had plenty of time to get the red out before she had to act as hostess for a hundred people.

Zoe never considered her mother to be an introvert, but she recognized that her lifestyle wasn't comfortable for everyone, so she generally kept to herself. For Harmony Clearwater, the scene in front of her could very well have been considered a circus with her as the ringmaster.

A borrowed casket lay at the end of a large room inside the funeral home. Willow had created a tri-folded poster board and covered it with pictures of Seth. Zoe had created the bulletins. Raine arranged the zillions of flowers sent for the occasion. Each of them commented about overwhelming lilies and roses that flanked either side of the casket.

The line of people waiting to offer their condolences to Zoe, her parents and sisters was disconcerting. It wound around the inside of the room and out the door. She expected her mother would check her watch throughout the evening, waiting for her chance to bolt out the back. Instead, she seemed flattered. She thanked each person for coming as if this was the real deal.

Which it wasn't.

This was a show. A fake. A showy, public circus. Her family would never have done this to Seth. If it weren't for the fact that they were waiting for his mystery lover to show, Zoe would be the one to hold the back door open for her mother.

Matt and a few other plain-clothes police officers stood in the doorways in their suits and ties. They looked stiff and out of place for funeral patrons. Or maybe that was just because she knew they wore guns beneath their jackets.

Dane was another story. She always preferred him in his khaki shorts and leather bracelets, but this. The entire Sun Trips Touring staff was here, and she couldn't stop staring at him, gawking really. He was beautiful. Did he have his suit tailored, or did it just fit him that well? It was the same khaki color she loved that blended with his sun kissed hair. The sun kissed hair that he'd tamed enough for the occasion to pass for a cover model.

The scent of leather mixed with sand and sea blew over her senses. As the youngest of the Clearwaters, Zoe stood at the end of the receiving line and could practically feel the calming sensation as Dane moved to stand next to her. He respected her need to keep their relationship a secret and made no attempt at any kind of physical contact.

"It's okay, you know," he said seemingly to the air.

Glancing around, making sure it was her he was talking to. "What's okay?"

"This." He gestured around the room like he might be talking about the stuffy, artificial funeral.

"I just feel awful for my mother, that's all. This woman better show up after making all of us endure this."

"You can still have a celebration of life for him. Just the family."

"Hell yes, we will. This is just wrong."

"Do you really think he would have minded? Your mother certainly doesn't seem to."

Zoe glanced to her parents. It was true, damn it. Her mother smiled and hugged and had something to say to each and every person. Zoe did little more than nod as people passed.

"It's also okay if this is hard for you. You don't have to like the finality or the crowd."

She didn't know whether or not she liked that he pegged her. Taking a cleansing breath through her nose, she exhaled slowly through her mouth, forcing herself to smile. This wasn't about her. This was for Seth.

Her feet minded. How do women stand in heels all day long? It had been three hours…almost the end of the visitation. Would his mistress show? Would the woman wait and show up instead for the funeral that followed?

"What if she doesn't show at all?" Zoe asked under her breath as she smiled for the owner of the island drug store.

"She'll show."

"How do you know?"

"Because I would."

She had to think about that for a few minutes just as the wife and sons of Zoe's high school business teacher offered their condolences. It wasn't completely fake, she decided. Her brother truly did die. They truly hadn't, yet, had any kind of closing ceremony to say their farewells. So, the casket was borrowed. It wasn't like they would have had an open casket ceremony anyway.

The crowd didn't seem to be any thinner at the end of the visitation than it was at the beginning. She had to lean over each time she checked to see if Matt remained at his post by the back door.

Dane elbowed her as a woman wearing sunglasses and a scarf around her head stepped from behind the School Superintendent and placed her hand on the corner of the casket. Zoe's eyes darted to Matt. He wasn't in his spot. She tried to act naturally but had no frigging way of knowing what that would look like. Instead, she elbowed Willow, who elbowed Raine. Two of the plain-clothes officers approached from a side door. The woman turned her head ever so slightly in Zoe's direction. Zoe couldn't see through the sunglasses but swore the woman was staring at her.

She couldn't help it, a small squeal came from her throat. Her face must have screamed, 'get her,' because the woman slipped around the casket and out a door behind the tallest tripod of flowers. There was a door behind the flowers? Surely, Matt knew this. That must be where he was…waiting for her. The woman was trapped. That had to be it.

Looking to Dane, she searched his face for the same conclusion. It wasn't there. The two plain-clothes officers darted behind the flowers after her.

Awkwardly, her family kept up their façade, although not nearly as convincingly. To hell with it. She took off behind the officers, around the borrowed casket, behind the floral display, and through the doorway. It led down a wide hallway. Frigging heels. She took the time to stop and kick them off, causing Dane to nearly fall over her.

"She's getting away," Zoe growled as she ditched the shoes and ran in her bare feet along the tile floor. The officers reached the end of the hallway long before she did. One went right and the other left. They didn't know which way she went?

When she reached the end herself, Zoe noticed the left was the way to some kind of prep area. The right was an exit door. If she was the woman, she would be escaping, not sticking around to look for formaldehyde. A bright setting sun blinded her momentarily as she stepped out onto a sidewalk and instantly dug a small stone into her left heel.

Limping, she made her way to the grass before scanning the area. Matt and three officers were at each corner of the property, checking underneath cars and behind trees.

No frigging way.

The funeral continued as if nothing happened. Zoe was definitely not cut out for this. Matt and his men scoured the area inside and out as the funeral director asked the remaining guests to please take their seats. By the time Zoe had retrieved her shoes and made it back to the viewing room, her parents and sisters had already taken their seats in the front row. She glanced down and noticed Raine and Willow were holding hands.

Willow.

What had Zoe been thinking? She hadn't been thinking. The funeral of Willow's husband was much like this one. Closed casket, reception line. Except his had representatives from the armed forces flanking the American flag-covered casket.

Slinking on the other side of Willow, Zoe clasped her sister's hand and noticed how she clenched their fingers. Dane left her to be alone with her family. She hadn't realized how much she'd turned him into a crutch these past few weeks. The chair next to her seemed far away and very empty.

People spoke about Seth. Some told stories, some were more like testimonies. His old roommate finished speaking of Seth's messy habits, his late nights, and earned a few laughs when he shared about his fascination with Luciana's Dowry. The man's eyes turned to her father's. They nodded once to each other, then the man backed away from the podium and returned to his chair.

Her father stood, paused, then pulled a folded paper from the inside of his suit jacket as he dragged his feet the long journey to the podium. It was Zoe's turn to squeeze Willow's fingers.

"Thank you all for coming. It means a lot to Harmony and me. We haven't always been the easiest family to understand. For Seth's sake, I hope I can bring some light to that."

Zoe hadn't understood how much her father had closed off since the death of his first-born. It occurred to her he'd just spoke more words than she'd heard him say in one sitting in over two years.

And he wasn't finished. "Harmony and I were sixteen and juniors in high school when we learned she was pregnant. We had a choice to make and it wasn't a popular one with our families. It was then we gave up the life we knew. She went to school in the day, I went in the evenings." His eyes reddened as he set his paper on the podium and looked to Zoe's mother. "And we never regretted a minute of it. We had no idea what to expect, but we embraced our new life. With no money and little support from either of our parents, we learned to use the earth for food and resources. So did Seth. He loved the island. The nature, the mystery. And, yes, he loved his search for mythical treasure." He paused to take a breath. Zoe clutched her dress in the middle of her chest like that might keep her heart from beating out of her chest.

"Raised by two teenagers, he could have ended up a big ball of trouble. Instead, he grew up to be a man who made us proud. He worked, supported himself, and he dearly loved his sisters. Thank you, Seth, wherever you are. You suffered an inexcusable fate, but we know you're smiling down on us now."

The room remained silent. The funeral director let the power of her father's declaration sink in just the right amount of time before he motioned for his ushers to begin dismissing the rows of people.

TWENTY

Zoe's mother reassured Matt a dozen times. Yet, he still argued that this could wait until morning, but—as far as police sketches go—the sooner the better. "I feel okay," she told him. "Better than okay, really. I can't explain it. All those people. They were wonderful. I had no idea how delightful that would feel. We were so young when we had Seth, I can't remember life before him. Now, I feel like I can move on. It's the strangest thing."

I can't remember my life before you came crying into my office. Dane. He was there for her. He followed her behind the funeral procession so they weren't seen together. He was her rock in an ocean of quicksand.

Chief Roberts was away at an antiques auction. Matt had taken it upon himself to use the conference room at the Ibis Island City Hall as a meeting place. Zoe would love to be a fly on the wall when the chief found out. That may be something cops did for one another in Reno or Chicago…maybe even St. Petersburg, but Ibis Island?

He'd called in 'his' sketch artist who met with each of them at the far end of the common area that held metal desks for the few officers Ibis Island had. One of the two who was on duty paced nervously. The other one was driving the streets, Zoe assumed. What did she know about these things?

The other officers Matt brought with him met with Raine, Willow and her parents, but Matt interviewed Zoe himself. "If this is the woman who attacked you, you might be able to recognize her. Her build? The way she moved? Think about it, Zoe. Tell me what you remember."

She remembered all right.

How could she so easily forgive someone who broke into her parents' home? Her home? Seth's old apartment? Zoe should tell him what she remembered, what she thought. But she didn't.

It was the letters.

Whoever wrote those letters wasn't a crazed murderer. She was a victim. A victim who loved Seth. A woman who Seth loved back. She couldn't rat her out. Wouldn't.

"I'm sorry, Matt. The person, if it even was a woman, came at me from behind. The lights were all off until after she ran out the front door. She seemed as scared as I was, I remember that now."

The way his eyes squinted made her want to hide. He sighed overtly and sat back in his chair. "Okay, Zoe. You got the best look at her out of all of us, so tell me what you saw."

He was recording their conversation. He'd made her agree to it beforehand. She felt guilty. Was she?

"I remember she wore sunglasses and a sheer scarf that covered her head and neck. Which would go along with what she said in her letters about being abused. Either that, or she didn't want anyone to recognize her. Her hair was brown, I think. It showed near her face...her forehead I mean." Did he notice she was giving only half-truths?

Miriam Roberts, the police chief's wife. Zoe could almost

swear to it. She was the right build, the right height, and Zoe remembered watching her when she staked out the police chief's house.

Holy shit. She staked out the Ibis Island chief of police's house. Who was a wife beater and very likely the man who murdered her brother. And now she was lying to a detective. She should be thrown in jail.

She couldn't look Matt in the eyes. Instead, she let them wander to the picture window leading into the conference room. He smiled at her. Dane's big, beautiful blue eyes smiled at her and all seemed right in the world. He was in love with her, couldn't remember life before her. And he donated millions of dollars' worth of treasure to the Smithsonian. He changed. People do that. It was a change she would have never expected.

"Zoe?" Matt spoke loudly.

"Huh? Oh, sorry. Just thinking. I'm really not clear on this, Matt, and I'm not comfortable guessing. I did some guessing after the break-in at my parents' home, and look what that got me. I will call you." She rested her hand on his forearm. "I will. If I think of anything you can use. I'll call you first thing."

He reached his other hand over and laid it on top of hers. Patting it twice, he added, "And if you think of anything you don't want me to know, Zoe? You do want me to solve this case, right? I may have pieces to a puzzle I can't tell you about. If you give me the other half of the piece, I might catch Seth's killer."

It wasn't necessarily a dirty move on his part, but it was effective, nonetheless. He tilted his head to her, making her positive that he had an ulterior motive, then shared one of his puzzle pieces. "There were fingerprints on the letters. Seth's, yours, each member of your family's were on the first letter, and a set of fingerprints we didn't find in our database."

Oh boy. "I'll think on it, Matt. Truly. Thank you for everything."

It killed Dane to drive separately. He'd even rented a Lexus for the night, because he didn't want Zoe to have to climb into his Jeep wearing her funeral dress. Now, he waited alone in her driveway because…why?

He was finished with discreet. His employees were going to respect their relationship or they could find other jobs. The head-lights of Henry's ancient Camry turned down her drive. The car stopped for several minutes. He couldn't see exactly who all was in there, but he noticed bodies as they leaned together and hugged.

She exited the car, stood for a moment like she'd had too much to drink, gained composure, then waved as the car backed out to the street and drove away. As she turned for the house, her head and shoulders dropped ever so slightly. Others might not notice, but he knew everything about Zoe Clearwater.

Realizing she didn't know he was in the car, he opened the door and paused, hoping not to startle her. She didn't jump, not even a twitch. That was a bad sign, coming from Zoe. Her feet stopped when he shut and locked the car. He stepped to her and wrapped his arms around her shoulders. She leaned her cheek on his chest, letting the weight rest on him. He wished she would let the weight of the rest of her body lay on him, too.

She turned and took his hand in a signal she was ready to head for the front door. "I could do something," she mumbled. "Why don't I do something?"

"Stop it." It came out more forcefully than he would have liked.

Her feet stopped short, and she turned to him, looking as surprised as he was at his tone. "You don't understand. You're not me."

This time he took her shoulders. "Stop. Enough. So, you

chose to be a responsible business owner two years ago to cover for a sick employee. It was Seth who chose to dive inexperienced and without a partner. It was his risk to bear, not yours. And who cares if you didn't realize your attacker was female at first? You're not a cop. You're a woman who was attacked in the safety of the home you grew up in. You're human, Zoe. A regular human who had a lot to get through today. Willow doesn't get to somehow trump the grief for your brother just because her husband died five years ago."

He reached down and kissed her once, feeling her shoulders melt under the palms of his hands. "I love you." He kissed her again. "I love everything about you." And once more. "Even when you make me want to shake you." Beneath his lips, her mouth expanded into a smile.

She pulled away, creating a breeze between them. It made her too damned far away. Her eyes turned a brighter green when she cried. The tears didn't escape this time. They pooled in her lids as she took his hands and placed one over each of her breasts. He went from control to crazed in seconds. She could do that to him. He grabbed hold as she pulled the shirt from his pants that didn't fit so well in his sudden condition.

She had strong hands for a woman. Years of maintaining boats and hauling diving equipment. Her fingers grabbed posses-sively at the muscles in his back as she lifted to her toes and smashed their lips together. Hers were needy and aggressive.

One of her thighs dipped between his as he adjusted his head and dove in deeper. What was his life like before Zoe? How had he lived with her so close for so many years and not seen? None of that mattered, now. He'd be damned if he let her slip by him again.

Taking into account the day she'd just endured, Dane decided to be the grown up. "We're in your driveway," he groaned.

"Mmm," she crooned and lifted the knee nuzzled between his legs. "Too bad I don't have any grass."

Painfully, he pushed away and took her hand, leading her to the front door. "Yeah. Sea shell mulch might be painful."

She pulled her tiny purse around and took out her keys. At least she was locking her door regularly, now. He pressed himself against her back, kissing her neck and wrapping his hands around her as she opened the door.

He smelled cigarettes.

A female voice came from deep in the house. "Don't turn on the lights." It was an older voice, raspy.

Fumes erupted from his insides. Zoe froze beneath his hands. Uncharacteristically, she didn't tremble. He maneuvered himself in front of her.

"No, Dane," Zoe said confidently and moved to stand next to him. "When I said I could do something…it was because today I figured out who this is."

What. The. Hell?

"You're Miriam Roberts," Zoe said and took a step forward.

The silence could've killed him. His eyes had adjusted to the dark back in the driveway. He could see the outline of a woman. She was small, but she had a gun. He was sure Zoe could see it, too. Why wasn't she scared?

A lighter flicked as Roberts brought it to the cigarette dangling from her lips. Her hand shook the lighter as much as the other one trembled with the gun.

"It doesn't matter, anyway." Roberts took a long drag, then reached down and turned on the table lamp. The glow beneath her chin sent an extra wave of awareness through him. This woman was the one who had broken into Zoe's home, the one who had attacked her at her parents'.

"I want the letters," Miriam said before taking a long drag.

"I'm leaving. You can tell my husband whatever you want. I don't care if he finds me."

Zoe held out her hands. "Let us help you."

Help her?

The woman's head jerked before she let out a laugh. "Help me? Do you mean help to put me away? I've planned this too long. Should have done it some time ago. But I wasn't sure..."

Slowly, Zoe sunk to the chair nearest the front door. Dane cringed as the shaking point of the gun followed her.

"Why now, Miriam?"

"You found him." Rubbing circles, she pressed the palm of the cigarette hand deep into the socket of one of her eyes. "I wasn't sure. When he was reported missing, I assumed he'd been murdered, but what if I had been wrong? I thought my husband had done it. I was sure of it. I should have shot him while he slept. You don't understand."

The light showed tears as they dripped freely down Roberts' face. "I didn't care if I died in the wake of Seth's disappearance. But I waited for him. Waited until I realized he wasn't coming for me, for us. I thought Neil had found out about us. That he killed Seth and was going to kill me. But then, time went on, and I realized Neil would have told me what he'd done, would have rubbed it in my face every day for the rest of my life. He would have never kept quiet about killing my lover."

Or maybe he didn't want to serve forty-five to life.

"Everything went on...like it always did. I honestly don't think it was Neil now." It was Miriam's turn to sink to the chair on the other side of the couch. She propped her leg up, took a drag and used her knee as a place to set the gun. "I want my letters. I want the only thing I have left in this world that means anything to me."

"Miriam. Dear. I can't get those for you."

Miriam lifted the gun and aimed it at Zoe's head. "You can, and you will."

Dane held up his hands, pleading. He judged whether he should jump between them or if the sudden movement would make Miriam shoot.

The grimace on her face turned to defeat as the shaking gun lowered slowly. Zoe grabbed Dane's thigh, holding him where he was.

Miriam began to cry more than just tears. She buried her face in her hands and sobbed. "I can't do it. Seth loved you. He spoke of you continually," she said into her hands. "I feel like I know you. I'm sorry I scared you that night in your parents' home. I didn't know what to do. I just want my pieces of him so I can disappear."

Zoe lifted from the chair and moved slowly to her. He flanked her side, and as she distracted the woman, he slipped the gun from the chair into the pocket of his pants. Miriam didn't notice but buried her head into Zoe's outstretched arms.

TWENTY-ONE

The craziness with Miriam Roberts took them late into the night. By the time things were settled, it was too late to sleep. Zoe had to walk the beach in the morning, so Dane convinced her to head out early. Middle of the night could be classified as morning when you're an Ibis Island native.

"It's well into July," she said as he took her warm hand in his.

He had to admit, the barefoot walk on smooth sand helped to bring some kind of clarity to the turn of events.

She continued as if nothing had happened. "It means we'll have both adults laying eggs and nests hatching almost nightly. Who needs sleep at a time like this?"

They walked her designated section of the beach, although she explained they would need to repeat the path again before the sun came up in case new activity happened between now and then.

Waves crashed next to them in the quick wind. The bubbly water threatened, lifted, then threw itself down before sending an inch of warm salt water up the sand to seep over their toes.

"I promised Matt," she confessed randomly. Had it been eating at her?

It was probably a good thing the dude's name no longer made him want to break something. "Promised?"

"He suspected something when he interviewed me."

"You're a rotten liar."

"It's true. I promised him I would share what I knew when I could."

"You should tell him."

She stopped and rotated her head, pointing innocent eyes to him that shone green in the night. "You're defending Detective Osborne?"

They hadn't changed from their dress clothes. He still wore his pants, rolled up to mid-calf, but had ditched the jacket and tie. She wore a coral dress that left her shoulders bare. The color mixed with the green, making her look like treasure.

"I plan to, once Miriam has a chance to get away," she said. "I can't begin to understand what she's been through. When the letters mentioned a powerful man, I hadn't imagined she meant a powerful man who had the connections to trace her every move. Her plan is genius, you have to admit."

"Miriam seemed as suspicious as Matt," she added as an afterthought.

He let his head fall back as he laughed. "Not many who point a gun at a woman after breaking and entering expect the victim to help them skip town."

With his back to the water, the angle of the beach made their height difference less pronounced.

"It feels right. I feel right." Turning, she took his other hand. "Thank you for being here through this. You've protected me and set me straight, at all the right times. You're good for me. But I'm keeping you from your life. You haven't been on a treasure hunt in forever or spent a single night at your place."

He let go of one of her hands, tucking the hair that blew in the wind over her golden shoulder. Her eyelids drifted closed and her head tilted back just enough to expose the side of her neck. "You are my treasure." He trailed his lips along her shoulder and up her neck to just behind her ear. "My place is wherever you are." She shivered as he took her earlobe in his teeth. He predicted the tremble and found himself looking forward to it.

She pushed him away and began working the buttons on his shirt. His fingers clenched her shoulders and her silky lips followed the release of each button. She was the only woman alive who could make him lose himself like this. She reached the last button and straightened, shoving his shirt over his shoulders before traveling her fingers inside the waist of his pants. His lungs emptied.

The rise in his senses took over, replacing coherent thought with instinct. He slipped off his shirt and opened it over the sand. Pulling the thin dress material from her shoulders, he ran his hands along her bare skin and let the tiny sounds of her moans echo the pulse of the waves.

The awe in her eyes as they traveled over the tattoo on his chest helped him slow to a reasonable pace. They had all night… or morning. He lowered himself to his knees, pulling the dress further, allowing the wind to cool the circles he made with his tongue. Her hands laced through his hair and took hold, pulling him closer. He ran his hands along her strong swimmer's thighs, searching, needing. He found her as ready for him as he was for her. The reaction to his touch was expected and yet potent. Nails dug into his shoulders as her legs buckled.

Placing one hand on her backside, he used the other to break her fall, lowering her to the soft ground. She lifted her dress over her head like a t-shirt, making him nearly choke. Her ease with nudity was every man's dream. But this woman was his alone. His forehead dropped to the middle of her. How could this be so different? She spread the dress next to his shirt and they rolled on their makeshift blanket. Her lips explored as he stripped away any last piece of material that kept him from her bronzed flesh.

"Look at you," he growled, making her writhe in bliss. "Perfect."

He could see the blush erupt on her already flushed face in the dim light of the hazy moon. "Come to me."

Needy hands grabbed and possessed him, hesitating only when her body shook and her voice cried out. "I love you," she moaned as she quivered in his hands. The need in her eyes bore holes into him as she let herself come down from the clouds.

Clothes lay strewn, just out of reach of the sneaky waves. She rolled, straddling him while small trembles still owned her. "Let's stay in this spot forever. We can eat like the Ibis and survive off of this." He wasn't ready. He wanted to make her climb again and again but she slipped over him so fast and complete, he lost any last ounce of reality. She was his in this moment. No one else could touch her, hurt her, have her. Grabbing her hips, he lifted and pulled. They moved like a machine racing to turn up the heat. He reached out his hands and she took them. They clasped fingers, and her knees dug into the sand near his sides. Her elbows locked, using him as purchase as they quickened.

Her eyes rolled to the back of her head, and he knew it would be soon. Taking a deep breath, he let himself go. Together, they swam in a turbulent sea of release, pulsing like the waves as they tried again and again to sink deeper.

The calm after the tsunami reminded him of an ocean sunrise. He wanted to pull her over him and sleep until the sun came up. Instead, she lifted her hands to the sky and cheered like she'd just won a five-hundred yard freestyle race.

"Holy shit, woman." He pulled her down and rotated until she was under him. "I'm in love with you." Ducking his lips beneath her ear, he tucked her into him.

"Just so you know," she whispered. "We make fun of people who do this."

He lifted his head to see if she was serious. "Have sex?"

"On the beach, yes."

He propped on his elbow, then checked down the beach one way before the other. "Do people do this often?"

"Are you telling me you've never had sex on the Ibis Island beach?"

"I am a beach sex virgin," he confessed. "Or I was. I think we shook the ground." He set his lips on the spot behind her ear and grinned as she shivered.

"We find naked people on the beach some mornings when we walk."

"Tourists." Not only were they invading their beaches, they were distracting his woman from after-sex bragging.

"Locals. Almost every one of them."

Now, he was distracted. "No shit?" He noticed her panties lying on the sand behind her head. He sat up and shook them out. "Do you think we'll get all the sand from our clothes?"

Sitting up next to him, she took them from his hand. "Absolutely." She indeed was a sea goddess. Her perky C cups taunted him. Grabbing the panties, he tossed them over his shoulder and lowered her to the ground, taking her again.

All six of them waited in the lobby at the St. Petersburg Police Department. Her family and Dane. Zoe watched as Matt stopped short at the sight of them. He mouthed the words, "Oh boy," as plain as day.

Zoe stood and held up a pleading hand.

Matt shook his head and asked, "Are they here for intimidation or support?"

"Support. One hundred percent support, I swear."

"Either way," he sighed. "Come on up."

He took them to St. Pete's equivalent of a conference room.

As they filed in, Zoe noticed they placed themselves in order of hierarchy. Matt stood. Her mother took the head, followed by her father, Raine, and Willow. She and Dane sat together at the end.

Matt didn't take lead. He leaned a shoulder next to an interactive white board and waited.

Fine.

"Miriam Roberts," she blurted out. None of her family flinched at her confession, of course, because they were Clearwaters. Each was privy to anything she knew.

Matt pushed from the wall. "Damn it, Zoe."

"I told you I'd tell you," she said more loudly than she'd intended. "I'm telling you."

He turned his mouth toward the radio thing on his shoulder. "Officer Louis, get in here." He walked to her and, ignoring Dane, leaned closer to her, pointing his finger in her face. "You knew."

"I *thought* I knew. Okay, okay, I was pretty sure I knew, maybe positive, but I...I'm sorry."

"Where is she?"

"Hiding."

"Where. Is. She?"

Defensive of her brother's lover...or maybe just for an abused woman, Zoe stood. "She didn't kill him. She loved him." It sounded ridiculous as she said it. "She just wanted their mementos so she could run away." Worse. "That's why she broke in. She didn't want to hurt me. She was as scared as I was."

"Do you think Chief..." He stopped and dipped his chin. She could see his jaw muscles flex and release. "Do you think if this woman is married to an abusive man, he might maybe hurt her if she tries to run away?"

"She knows what she's doing."

"She said she didn't care if he found her." It was Dane. Oh, no. He was right. She'd said that. Chief Roberts was a chief. He would know how to find her.

Her lungs began to pump as she sunk back into her chair. The officer Matt had called slipped in the back of the room.

"We can't prosecute Mrs. Roberts for breaking into your home if you don't press charges. Tell me where she is, Zoe."

"I don't know exactly. She told me she had a fake ID. Jane Smith."

"Jane Smith?" he repeated sarcastically.

"She showed us the ID. She was headed inland. Where she went to college. She knows a professor. That's all she said."

Dane taught a diving class the next morning. It was hard to watch him leave. Zoe yearned to take a group down, at least for a tour if not a certification.

He used his hips and pressed her against the back of her front door. "Come with me."

It wasn't exactly the same context as when he used those words the night before, but it still made her shiver. "I have things to do." Lie. "What if Matt needs me for something about Miriam? And I captain the snorkeling boat this afternoon. I'll see you in between."

He kissed her slow and lazy. "I could get used to this," he whispered in her ear.

"I...suppose you don't necessarily need to be here anymore. The person who broke into my home is gone." Why couldn't she leave well enough alone? "You need to get to work. I shouldn't have brought it up."

"Are you asking me to leave?"

"No!" she said pathetically.

"Then, I'll see you between shifts." He kissed her forehead much like he'd done dozens of times before, but this time seemed different. Important.

Peeking out the corner of her window, she watched his Jeep turn from the drive onto her street. She shook her head in disbelief at the changes in her life. As she turned to head toward the kitchen, she noticed lights flashing on every inch of her walls. Spinning, she ran back to the window, counting six police cars as they squeezed into her drive and on her sea shell mulch.

Her first thought was that something happened. An emergency. She ran out the door to ask if anyone was hurt and noticed Chief Roberts. Chief Roberts who never showed his face anywhere. Her feet froze to the spot on her drive. They wanted to run. Miriam's abusive husband was walking toward her, slow and cocky. But, there were other officers. Surely he couldn't hurt her if there were other officers. It looked as if the entire Ibis Island police force was there.

"Miss Clearwater," Chief Roberts drawled. "I hate to make a house call under such awful circumstances."

As if he ever made a house call before in his life.

"We have a warrant, here, to search your house for a person wanted on the murder of one Seth Clearwater. The suspect was last seen escaping with you at a funeral two days ago."

He knows. Her mind was a blur of possibilities. Could he arrest her? Take her? He must not know where Miriam was hiding. Or did he and this was a ruse?

She knew each of the officers, of course. She tried to offer some sort of greeting as they passed, but her voice wouldn't work. The looks on most of their faces were that of embarrassment or sympathy. A few said they were simply disgusted.

Maybe this would be fast. And then she could get in her Jeep and run to Dane before he pushed off.

Loud noises erupted from inside her house, making Zoe twirl in that direction. A hand clamped down on her forearm. The pain was immediate and caused her body to give in the direction of the grip.

The chief's smile was all-knowing, and it scared her enough to make her forget about her arm. "You want to stay right where you are, little lady."

TWENTY-TWO

Dane sped down the ten mile long, two-lane road that led from Sun Trips pier through the island. He turned in the middle, heading toward Zoe's house. Greg said she called in sick. He'd just seen her that morning. She wasn't sick, and she wouldn't answer her phone.

He spun into her drive, skidding to a stop behind her Jeep, and threw on the emergency brake. The front door was opened wide. As he jogged toward it, he could see her. She sat on the couch with her legs crossed and her eyes closed. She was meditating? As soon as he stepped inside he saw why she was 'sick.'

The couch was the only thing in the house that was upright. Papers littered the floors. Furniture was overturned. The hallway leading to the back bedrooms was filled with dresser drawers and clothing. He knelt down beside her, gently taking her hands.

Her eyes opened. They were dilated. How long had she been sitting like this? Her pupils shrunk to normal as soon as her gaze landed on his. "You came for me." She smiled.

"Of course I came. What the hell happened?"

"I think we're in trouble." She placed her hands on the sides of her neck. "Chief Roberts was here."

"What? Are you hurt?" He looked her over and noticed a ring around her forearm. Four red marks distinctly resembled fingers.

She shook her head. "It's no use. He knows. He thought she might be here. He's looking for her. He knows I know."

"Have you called anyone? Matt? Your family?" Why hadn't she called him?

She shook her head again. "He made his rounds to each of our homes. They all look like this. I haven't called Matt. You came for me," she repeated.

"I did. Let's get you out of here. We can go to my place."

She shook her head for a third time. "Maybe later. I'm better. Greg is going to cover for me."

"He told me."

Her eyes darted to his. "Did you tell him you were coming here?"

Was she seriously asking this? "Why didn't you call me?"

"I'm better," she repeated. "You were right, what you said about me. I work to find answers, and I am determined." She untwisted her legs from the contortion she'd had them in and placed them gently on the floor. "Chief Roberts wants to scare me, to scare my family." She moved her glance over the destruction around her. "He doesn't understand that this," she held out her arms, "means nothing to us. We are all unharmed."

He wondered if she realized how she rubbed the ring around her arm after she said that.

"And we're damned pissed off about our brother. He did it, Dane. I can feel it."

"You're a complicated woman. I'm in love with you, and I'm proud." He splayed his hand on the side of her face, brushing his thumb across her soft cheek. "And if you don't call me next time you're in trouble I'm going to handcuff you to me."

Her brows lifted high. "I might not hate that."

"Come." He stood and pulled her next to him, digging in her pocket for her phone. "You need to call Matt, then we should get over to Harmony and Henry. See if they need us."

He found Matt's number under 'Osborne, Detective,' then placed the phone in her hand.

"We made an agreement. We all clean up our own places, then move to whoever isn't done. Mine and Raine's will be the quickest. We don't have much stuff. Willow and my parents' will be another story." She took her phone-free hand and placed it on his jaw. "I have you to thank for much of this."

He knew she didn't mean the mess, but it made him huff out a breath anyway.

"I mean that you give me strength I didn't know I had. I love you, too."

The strength was already there. She just needed to unbury it from beneath the rest. But he wasn't about to relinquish the compliment. "All right. Let's get busy." He surveyed the place as she called Osborne.

He could hear him on the other end of Zoe's cell.

"Yeah, I'm nearly to your place now," he said.

"Now? How?" she asked.

"Your mother and Willow called. What a cluster."

"I know the other half of that saying, Matt." She was making jokes when her house was just vandalized by a corrupt cop and his cronies.

"Yeah, well you're a lady. I'm in the drive."

Zoe slid the phone back into her pocket.

Dane had the two end tables and chairs righted before he got to the door. It was open, but Osborne tapped on it as he walked through.

He looked around and shook his head. "Is anything broken?"

Zoe lowered her brows as if she hadn't thought of it. "I don't think so."

"Let me see your copy of the warrant while you take a look around and see, please."

Purposely, Dane let her check out her place without him as he stayed back with Osborne. "You think it's an illegal search?"

"Not illegal, necessarily. But he's got connections somewhere. The same judge signed each warrant, which isn't unusual in itself. I just can't imagine what he said to the judge to get him to sign."

Dane found himself thinking out loud. "And if he trashes the Clearwater homes without breaking anything, they can't file a complaint."

"You're smarter than you look."

"You're an asshole."

"Glad we cleared that up."

Zoe's eyes moved between him and Osborne as she reentered the room. "Nothing that I can see. My drawers are overturned and on the floors. Closets, too. But nothing that can't be straightened out."

Osborne nodded.

"He must really want his wife back." Dane wasn't sure if he was asking a question or making an observation.

"Yeah," Zoe agreed. "And I don't like the reason why. Have you found any trace of her, Matt?"

He shook his head as he placed her lamp back on an end table. "We found record of her at a junior college in Destin, but her class schedule is long gone. I've got some guys checking out professors who worked in her field of education at the time she was enrolled. We don't think she's in Destin."

Working as a team, the three Clearwater homes were put back together in no time. Following Matt's request, Zoe made sure everyone agreed to meet and discuss the 'searches.' They needed to get on the same page regarding how to handle Chief Roberts. Since it was early in the week and still mid-afternoon, they decided on Willow's bar. All five Clearwaters were there, Dane, Matt and even Chloe. Liam had moved the jukebox in front of the sheet of dangling plastic that hid his construction of Willow's dance floor. Dane loaded it with a zillion dollars' worth of songs. They listened as they made plans around three round tables clustered together.

"Everyone needs to travel in groups," Matt ordered. "Never less than two. The more the better. It's possible he might to try and corner you. The way he tossed your homes indicates a probable goal of intimidation. That would follow the overall personality profile of an abuser. Unfortunately, he's also a police chief. He may think he's above the law. To a point, maybe he is. That is, unless you're together. Then there's a witness. Raine, I want you to stay at your parents'."

Raine nearly spit out her beer. "You're not telling me what to do."

Matt ran his hands over his face. "Let me rephrase, oh mighty princess."

Zoe couldn't help it. She laughed so hard she *did* spit out her beer. Matt must've been at the end of his patience. He started in on his rephrasing but by that time her mother and father had joined in with the laughter. Chloe probably didn't know what was so funny, but she took one look at her grandpa laughing and joined in.

Raine's face transformed into something between a tomato and a lobster. Since she'd never blushed a day in her life, Zoe knew it was good old-fashioned pissed off. Matt wasn't laughing, either.

Killjoys.

When the laughter died down enough so he could be heard, Matt rephrased for the princess. "Is there someone you could stay with so you're not alone? Willow? Your folks? An axe murderer?"

She squinted, leaned back, and set her arm on the back of Willow's chair. "What do you think, Willow? You want a roomie for a day or two?"

Matt leaned forward as Raine leaned back. "Or a week or two."

"Fine."

"Fine."

"Children. Children." Her mother waved a hand between them. "I propose a toast."

Really?

"I toast the perseverance of the Clearwaters. And the dedication of our new friend, Detective Osborne." Her mother waited a moment, then added, "Lift your glass, Raine, dear."

Raine obeyed, of course. A round of clinking glass resonated.

Dane took Zoe's hand. "May I have this dance?"

"There's um, no dancing here."

"There is now, babe," he said as he pulled her to her feet.

The song was slow. In fact, they all were.

He tugged one of the belt loops at the front of her jeans, pressing their hips together. The red in her cheeks wasn't from good old-fashioned pissed off.

"You're different," he said as he guided their joined hips in a dance that was nothing short of foreplay. Was she supposed to carry on a lucid conversation when he did this?

"H-how so?"

Dipping his lips to her ear, he let them brush against her as he answered. "Confident. Calm. Collected. And sexy as hell, but that last part's not different."

Damn it if she didn't shiver in the warm room.

"You just haven't had sex in," she looked at an imaginary watch on her wrist, "almost twenty-four hours."

"Ouch," he whispered and kissed her bare shoulder. She let her arms slide up his back and her hips follow his as they moved in their tiny circle near the jukebox.

He crooned in her ear the way he did when they made love. "I guess we'll have to be glue for the next day or two."

"Or week or two," she amended.

The song ended and they broke apart, returning to the loud table. Everyone planned their logistics of who stayed with whom and how they would handle Turtle Conservation calls.

"Are you guys gonna have a baby, now?" Chloe didn't say it loud, but the table stopped their conversations as if someone had turned off a switch.

"Um," Zoe said, looking around at the eyes that were all trained on her. "Why would you ask something like that, sweetie?"

Chloe shrugged. She seemed to sense she was the reason for the sudden silence. "You put your bodies together." She gestured to the spot they were dancing. "Mom says that's how you have babies."

"Willow Clearwater," her mother barked.

Uh oh. Zoe wanted so badly to shout out an 'Ooo,' but didn't for Chloe's sake.

Her mother actually pushed away from the table and stood. Ouch. "You mean to tell me you haven't explained about human bodies and sex to my granddaughter?"

Zoe thought she remembered her first 'talk' before she hit pre-school...and refresher courses several times after.

"Mom. She's six years old."

"She's asking, isn't she? I'll just have to do it for you."

"No!" Zoe and her sisters yelled all at once.

TWENTY-THREE

Dane was part scared shitless and part excited as hell. He wanted this to be right, and he wanted Zoe. And not just for a week or two. It had been several days since Roberts tore up the Clearwaters' homes. The time was never going to be right, so he was just going to do it.

Taking a deep breath, he stepped through the door of the best jewelry store this side of the peninsula. And he would know these things. Larue's was known for the quality and variety of their stones and the flexibility of settings. He knew exactly what he wanted. Circle diamond. Larue quality. The best. Not too big. Maybe a karat. With a single smaller diamond on each side. The two of them becoming one. He could give a shit if it was stupid. He was stupid in love. He'd admit it to anyone.

He'd arranged for her to assist Liam on a bigger scuba tour. She agreed, but only as the driver. Small steps.

The inland mall was home to three jewelry stores, a handful of larger chain clothing stores and a scattering of traditional, Florida local shops with a Greyhound bus stop at the end so arriving tourists could spend money first, find a place to stay later.

He worked the poor salesman until he had him almost in tears. Dane knew his gemstones and wasn't paying a penny more than he should. He decided on yellow gold. It wasn't what the girls were wearing for jewelry, but he was a treasure hunter and white gold just wouldn't fit. They fit. With her, he was a man. He was whole. He would ask her and, if needed, drag her off to the nearest deserted island and make her say yes.

The diamond he picked wasn't from the bag of stones the salesman shook out into the velvet-bottomed tray in the back room. It was in the display case. Speaking to him. A few metaphorical tears later from the salesman and Dane had one solitaire engagement ring in his pocket. It felt more right than anything he'd done in his life. A local cheese and cracker shop was on the way to where he parked his Jeep. He chose an extra sharp cheddar with some fancy cracker thing the gal behind the counter recommended. A reputable liquor store carried the proper wine for such an occasion. The salmon filets and bakers already waited in the fridge.

She would say yes, wouldn't she? He started to worry as he walked to the parking lot. Of course she would, he decided, as he glanced in the bus stop. His feet stopped before the rest of him, causing him to throw his arms out so he wouldn't fall and crush his cheese and crackers. He jutted his chin closer to the window as if that would make a difference. His eyes zeroed in on the cork bulletin board next to the ticket counter.

Wanted: Miriam Roberts.

He didn't watch where he was going as he kept his eyes on the 8" x 11" piece of paper like it might disappear if he blinked. Nearly running into an elderly woman on his way in, he made himself pay attention, apologize and hold the door for her before he passed through.

Wanted: Miriam Roberts. For murder. Do not attempt to approach. Is considered armed and dangerous. Call the Ibis Island Police Department if you have information leading to the arrest of this suspect.

Dane had been quiet the entire ride back to Zoe's house. Granted, the entire ride from Sun Trips was a whopping five minutes, but she expected him to riddle her with questions about her first scuba tour in over two years. Well, not tour so much as driving a boat for Liam's tour. But still.

She'd been talking incessantly about the couple who dove together that reminded Zoe of her and Seth. They leaned toward the plant and animal life versus the shipwrecks and caverns.

She would keep herself from acting petty and think about food. Had she eaten lunch? "Don't tell Mom and Dad, but I think I want steak tonight."

That got his attention. He nearly ran over her mailbox, craning his head at her as he pulled into her drive.

"Just kidding. I wasn't sure if you were paying attention."

"Of course I was. I'm a dude, babe."

His sarcasm warmed her heart. Along with the nickname that irritated the hell out of her not long ago. How could this feel so right? Dane Corbin?

He pulled a paper bag she hadn't noticed from the back of his Jeep. As casually as she could, she said, "I'm going to hit the shower before starting dinner. Care to join me?" She loved the way his feet ground to a halt in the gravel. It was only a moment before he continued his trek, but it was worth it.

"Rain check?" he asked.

…and her bubble burst. No pouting, Zoe. She wasn't in love with a machine.

"I picked up some things," he amended. "I'm making dinner tonight."

Bubble securely back in place, she kissed him on the cheek as she unlocked her door. Keys on the rack, shoes by the door. She took no more than two steps toward her bathroom before she smelled it. Cigarette smoke and a musky perfume.

Dane must have smelled it, too, because he set his bag down slowly and stepped in front of her.

A woman with short, jet black hair stepped out of the kitchen. "Hello, Dane. Zoe."

Miriam Roberts had long, blonde hair. Or at least she did the last time Zoe saw her. And this was definitely Miriam Roberts.

This time, Zoe didn't feel the same relief about finding this woman that everyone was looking for.

"What are you doing here?" Dane asked, still standing between Miriam and her.

"I see you've seen the posters." She took a long drag on her cigarette, gesturing to a corner of a paper sticking out of his grocery bag.

Posters? What posters?

"Everyone's looking for you," he said softly. "You come back to Ibis?"

Miriam sighed overtly. "The canary hiding in the cat's bed."

"What posters?" No one was offering an explanation.

Making her way toward them, Miriam explained. "My husband has put out a warrant for my arrest. An APB and all that."

"What the hell for?"

"For the murder of your brother. The small print reads that my husband has evidence I killed Seth. I'm armed and danger- ous." She looked positively spent. Maybe it was the way the black hair drained her face of any color. Or maybe it was because her face *was* drained of all color. "I'm sorry for bringing this to you. I didn't know where else to go. The professor I was staying with said he thought he was followed. He probably was."

It could have been Matt's men as easily as Chief Roberts.

"We're calling Detective Osborne," Dane said flatly. It was the first time she could remember him calling Matt by his formal title.

Miriam collapsed into the chair nearest the kitchen. She took another drag on her cigarette and, this time, Zoe noticed the way her hand shook. "I understand. Of course. Will you...give me time to get away?"

"No," Zoe pleaded. "He's a good cop. He wants to help you."

Zoe never thought anyone could be more suspicious of the police than Raine, but the look on Miriam's face said she trumped Raine tenfold. "Please, Miriam. Trust me. He thinks your husband used crooked warrants to trash our homes—"

"He searched your homes?"

Zoe nodded, then offered, "He didn't break anything."

Placing her face in her hands, Miriam broke. "I'm so sorry. I didn't know where else to go. What to do. I should just let him have me. It's only a matter of time. He has too many connections. You can't imagine."

"Please, Miriam. Let us call Detective Osborne."

Dane pulled out his cell. "There is no, 'let us.'"

Matt brought a plain-clothes police officer with him. Or maybe it was a detective. Zoe didn't know. She was more focused on Miriam. Her heart ached for her. She'd never seen a woman so emotionally bruised. Zoe's entire house smelled like the townie bar where no one followed the no smoking rules. She didn't have it in her to tell Miriam not to smoke.

Miriam didn't offer her side of the story. She didn't argue

about the murder accusation. She seemed to have simply shut down.

"You're not safe here," Matt said. "Patrols regularly check each of the Clearwater homes."

"I wasn't followed." Miriam must have seen the doubt in Matt's eyes as easily as Zoe did because she added, "I've been married to Neil for almost fifteen years. I know what I'm doing."

Matt nodded. "You've stayed off the radar for a long time."

"That time was coming to an end."

"What makes you think so?"

"The professor who hid me noticed he was being followed."

Zoe interrupted. "Was it you?" she asked Matt.

Matt shook his head. "We hadn't gotten that far. Which means if it is the chief, he's faster and knows more than we thought he did. The email attached to the arrest warrant bulletin reads that Roberts will stand witness to seeing you at the dive site the day Seth was murdered."

Miriam stood now, tossing her cigarette into a mug. "As if I could do that to anyone. Let alone Seth."

"How can this be?" Zoe blurted. Pent up frustration ate at her. "How can he sleep in his bed every night after what he did to my brother? What he did—is doing—to his wife?"

Dane squeezed her hand. It helped. It always helped. "She can stay at my place," he said.

Everyone turned to him.

"Think about it," he added. "Zoe has been neurotic about keeping our relationship under wraps. Other than the fact that Zoe works for me, no one on the island has any idea there is a connection between me and the Clearwater family."

Matt shook his head. "Your Jeep isn't exactly covert, Dane. It's been parked every night in front of Zoe's house for over a month."

"Look out the window," Dane suggested.

"What?"

"Look out the window. It's parked in back of the bushes. You can't see if from the street. I've checked."

He did that for her?

Matt looked out the window, then shook his head again anyway.

Dane didn't quit. "I was gone the day Roberts came with his gang and tossed Zoe's house."

Matt turned to her. "Zoe?"

Oh sheesh, he was asking her. So much rested on this. She stood and strolled to the window on the opposite side of the room. They'd danced a few times in public. But Dane Corbin had a reputation of doing that with everyone. "I think he might be right. Here's not safe. I could pull my blinds, but that would be obvious. I never do that. It would be easy to do at Dane's place, because no one has lived there in so long. Miriam?"

"I am thankful, truly I am. I'm also ready to accept the inevitable."

"Which is what?" Zoe raised her voice. "After all this, you're going to give up? After all these years? After Seth was willing to give up...his family for you?"

"I'm so sorry, Zoe. Please forgive me."

She did. She truly did. For it all. Zoe wrapped her arms around Miriam. Her hair reeked of smoke. It was masked only slightly by the scent of her musky perfume. This poor woman.

Pulling away, Zoe looked her brother's lover in the eyes. They were a pretty hazel. Warm. "Stay at Dane's for now, Miriam. It's perfect."

TWENTY-FOUR

The marine laboratory was nearly sixty miles south of Ibis Island. The sun was coming up on the left side of Dane's Jeep as he made the turn down the road that led to the staff only parking lot. Zoe sat crooked next to him, turned so she could see Willow in the back seat. They spoke of sea turtle stats, some comeback that started a few years ago, and about a dude who seemed to be the originator of sea turtle conservation. Zoe's beautiful voice was contagious and reminded him of the ring that rested in his pocket.

A nearly mature loggerhead was going to be released just after sunrise. It had been fitted with some sort of satellite thing on its back. Zoe tried to explain it to Dane as she got ready that morning.

He'd woken to an empty bed. All he would have needed to do was give his mind a chance to wake so he could remember today was the day to watch the turtle release. But with cold sheets next to him, it was hard to focus on anything but the empty space. The idea of not having her with him each morning felt like losing his right arm. The few seconds before his brain was fully awake

202

were unsettling enough that he nearly proposed to her as she came out of the shower.

There weren't a lot of options of where to hide a ring when wearing boxer briefs. And he had decided a bed head and bags under his eyes wouldn't make for a decent proposal.

Chloe sat next to Willow in his back seat. He could sense the buzz in the air as he found a place to park. He chose a spot next to Liam who rode with Henry and Harmony in Raine's SUV.

The biologist gal was there to greet them. Before they departed for the designated docking pier, she offered to give them a quick look-around. She spoke like a Sun Trips tour guide.

"In the first four tanks, we have two injured and two sick loggerheads."

Tanks? They were more like individual, above ground swimming pools.

"In the final tank is Milly. She's our only manatee at this time. They are docile animals and are often hit by boats. This one sustained especially deep cuts. See how the wounds are parallel lines? Each line is from the propeller of a boat as it traveled over her."

The animal was covered in more scars than just the ones she described. Most of them seemed like older wounds, but he wasn't about to ask.

"I'm afraid we don't let humans observe the dolphins up close. We don't want them to become accustomed to people."

Two biologists sat on a blanket on the floor in a corner. They were injecting some kind of fluid into the shoulders of a juvenile sea turtle. Dane supposed there weren't many places to inject much of anything when you're covered in a shell.

Another small group of biologists was pulling up the corners of the blanket under another turtle. They hoisted it up, secured it to a dangling hook and let go. The scale read one hundred ninety-five pounds.

The drive to the pier was short. They probably could have walked if not for transporting the sea turtle.

"We have 1,115 turtles attached with satellites. This one will be number 1,116."

The contraption looked like a tiny alien ship glued high up on the back of the turtle's shell. Genius. Not too tall. The biologist paused her explanation and grunted as she and another dude unloaded the turtle from the back of a truck. Dane took pride in remembering just how hard that was.

"The satellites have taught us that Gulf sea turtles migrate in circles all the way to the west coast of Africa and back again to within five to seven miles of where they were born. This is a male. Hopefully, this will be his last time on land. The females are the only ones that come out of the water and that's not until they're at least thirty years old when they are ready to lay eggs." As Raine recorded the show on her phone, the biologist and her assistant set the turtle on the sand. He might have been over empathizing, but Dane swore it knew. His flippers were pumping before his belly hit the sand. He headed straight for the water like his life depended on it. Dane guessed it did.

Be free, Dane thought. Without the satellite, no one would ever find him again. The biologist had her head buried in the portable instruments showing the turtle's location and video feed of what was in front of it.

Dane's eyes darted to Zoe. She was preoccupied, staring at the calm water where the turtle had disappeared. Had disappeared. In the Gulf. Where no one would ever find him. Why hadn't he thought of this?

Miriam Roberts sat in the driver's seat of a white rental sedan. Zoe realized that although she must be used to hiding out by now, this seemed different. The Florida Keys. Why should Zoe get to enjoy diving in North America's only natural coral reef while Miriam was holed up in a hotel room? Oh, right. Because Zoe didn't have an abusive cop husband searching frantically for her.

And to think the Florida Keys were somehow the consolation destination. Dane tried feverishly to talk them into hiding around the waters off the coast of Australia. Zoe had to agree the general idea was a good one. Get them all away from Ibis while Matt did his thing. But there was no way she was going all the way to Australia when Seth's murder was this close to being solved. And no cell phone service? Not going to happen.

Miriam wasn't a diver and emphasized her refusal to step foot on the modest speed boat they'd rented. Zoe hoped the rental car didn't have a no smoking clause as Miriam lit one up. "I'll be fine," Miriam assured her as she exhaled. "Maybe I'll spend some time at the pool. I have a handful of books I brought with me."

"Okay, but use the prepaid cell if you need anything at all," Zoe said. "We won't dive longer than an hour and will check our phones before and after."

It was a bit like watching Mom drive away as Zoe was left alone with a teenage boyfriend. Except Zoe would have never wanted Dane as a boyfriend when they were teenagers. She turned to watch him load the boat with the scuba gear they'd brought. He wore his swim trunks, a pair of leather sandals, and a Sun Trips t-shirt. She smiled as she gave herself a moment to think about what was underneath.

The tattoo on his left bicep flexed as he lifted. His brows dug low and he seemed to be mentally ticking off some invisible check list. She adjusted the strap on her cowboy hat and dug in to help. Dane did a point check of the boat and started her up.

No one grew up an Ibis native without diving the Florida

Keys, but this…This was with Dane, the childhood nemesis she'd somehow fallen hopelessly in love with. She untied the boat and snuggled into the passenger seat as he trolled away. No, it wasn't Australia and they wouldn't unearth any historical treasure, but she would damned well do the best she could to make the trip worth it.

The hat protected her face and neck, but she spread sunscreen there and everywhere else anyway. The breeze was gloriously scorching already at mid-morning.

The empty anchored boats they passed told her divers were already enjoying the coral. Privacy was something they wouldn't enjoy. It made her think of the incredibly sexy non-sex they had when he found her by Seth's cavern. Turning her head, she watched as his hair whipped in the wind. He sensed her gaze, tilted his head toward her and winked. It sent a shiver over her just as potent as the first time he winked at her.

They'd spent the last several weeks living side-by-side. Effort-lessly, they maneuvered around each other, in her kitchen, the bathroom, the bedroom. The bed. It was like a seamless dance between two people working as a team.

He was good for her. He was good, period. A good man she and Raine had pegged early on and let those preconceived notions stick for as long as they deemed necessary. Oh, the time she had wasted. But he was hers now. He loved her, crooned it in her ear dozens, maybe hundreds of times now. A rush of serenity washed over her.

"Here?" she asked and glanced around as he killed the engine.

"It looks like this is as private as we're going to get, and I see some movement down there. Let's go find out what it is."

Standing, she slipped off her shorts and pulled off her cowboy hat.

"Or," he amended, "we could stay here and get warmed up first."

How could he still make her blush? And in this heat? "There is no down-below on this boat."

"Babe." He pouted like an incredibly sexy, pouty, treasure hunting scuba diver.

As cruelly as she could, she slid her tank up and over her shoulders, giving her best impression of a lingerie model in a photo shoot. He dropped to his knees in front of her and placed his hands on the backs of her thighs.

"Dane," she said as she looked around. There were several boats within eye shot. "I was kidding."

"These are not funny," he said, looking to one of her breasts, then the other.

As she pushed him away, he fell back on his heels. He made no attempt to get his own gear and continued watching her.

"Watching you gear up is nearly as sexy. When are you going to teach again?"

Her eyes closed at his sudden change in subject. She pulled her air tank pack over one shoulder, then the other before fastening it around her waist. "We'll see."

She checked her safety points once, twice. Then, sat on the edge of the boat. Dane's safety checks were both seamless and subconscious. Together, they tipped backward and fell into the warm, salty waters. The wildlife was numerous and colorful. They dove nearly sixty feet and hovered near a cluster of anemones and the clown fish that called the poisonous creatures home.

They kicked their fins with yards between them, yet she constantly knew where he was. She adored how many of the live organisms had been given names due to their unscientific appearance. Lazily their fins brushed the tops of elkhorn corals. A group of brain corals sat to the north of them. A vast cluster of lettuce corals gathered beyond the brain coral.

She placed her hand through the pristine water and into one of the brilliantly colored schools of fish. The fish scattered outward like coral polyps. Turning her head to check on Dane's location, she found him watching her. Like he did on the boat ride out, he winked, then pointed upward. They needed to keep their trip short for Miriam's sake.

The stops at the designated ascension depths weren't as sexual, but somehow just as powerful. They spent their idling silent minutes reading each other's expressions. The blue in his eyes said serenity to her. She was in love and after growing up on the same island, yet miles apart, could never imagine life without him again.

Close to the surface, their final stop was bright with brilliant sunlight. He held out his hand and opened his pruney fingers. She held up hers, placing her fingers against his. Like the many dances they had now shared, their legs kicked, keeping them at the proper depth without banging knees.

When they broke the surface, she hooted aloud at a successful dive. But Dane wasn't facing her. She looked to see what captured his attention and noticed a man in a nearby boat waving them down. Dane had swum on his college team and was able to reach the boat long before she did. He was on board with his hands on each of the man's shoulders as she reached them. Dane worked to calm the man down and she was able to put the pieces together. The man had lost track of his diving partner. His teenage son. The Coast Guard was on its way, but the man wanted Dane to go back down with him. She watched as Dane asked all the right questions. How long had the boy been down? What depth? About where did the man last see his son?

Zoe dipped her head toward the bottom, lifted her feet in the air and let her weight sink before she began pumping her legs.

Dane would catch up. She had plenty of air. Plenty of time to find a single diver as long as the boy hadn't wandered off.

She passed an extensive cluster of clubbed finger coral before she spotted Dane. He nodded his head in acknowledgement and checked his way. A head stuck out from between two larger hill formations. Surely, the boy wasn't hiding, was he?

Cautiously, she approached him. As she looked around, she determined he was definitely alone and looked to be the right age. Placing her hands up, she faced her palms to him as she approached.

He was shaking and holding one of his legs. Between his fingers, blood oozed from a cut. The corals could be sharp as knives. The boy pointed up. A single bull shark circled far above. Bull sharks were small and could be aggressive. Generally, she would teach her scuba diving students to keep a wide berth from any shark and simply keep an eye on it. If divers didn't tease them or try to feed them, an attack was extremely rare.

This boy either didn't have that lesson or was terrified his bleeding leg might cause an attack. She supposed it was a possibility.

Dane looked to the boy, moved his glance to the shark, then back to the boy. He pulled a knife from his waist and swam ahead of them. Zoe was sure it was meant only to reassure the boy and yet…

She lifted the kid's air gauge, checked the level. It read empty. How long had he been down here? Bubbles continued to escape his breathing apparatus telling her that although his time may be up soon, it wasn't yet. Her eyes moved to the boy's. Tears pooled in his face mask.

She checked her depth device. Fifty feet. Keeping an eye on Dane and the shark, she took hold of the boy and guided him from his hiding place. Together, they rose to twenty-five feet and stopped just as his bubbles died. She grabbed his shoulders hard before the panic she read in his eyes had a chance to consume him. She removed her mouthpiece and turned it, setting it in front of his mouth. He spit out his mouthpiece and grabbed Zoe's. He took two slow breaths. She was infinitely impressed. The boy's fingers clamped her forearms, but he remembered his certification training. Keep calm. Take slow, shallow breaths.

They took turns taking two breaths until it was time to lift to ten feet, where they began to repeat the procedure. Two sharks. No, three. It was her turn to remember her certification training. The boy's father's boat was close enough that she could see the dad hanging over the side, waving his arms. The sharks didn't circle, didn't show any signs of agitation but certainly had smelled the blood. She decided the danger of the sharks trumped decompression sickness. Dane may have been having fun swimming near danger, but she wasn't taking any chances.

She tugged on the boy and swam using as little movement as possible. The boy was a lanky teenager, but he was full grown. His father pulled him into the boat—tank and all—as if he was as light as a toddler.

She turned to check on Dane. He was nearly to her. Shit, he was fast. Sounds of joyous cries erupted from the teen and his father as she and Dane headed away from their boat.

TWENTY-FIVE

Dane grabbed Zoe and put distance between them and the man's boat before the Coast Guard arrived with their questions and forms. When they returned to the boat he'd rented, he first unlocked the glove box and checked his phone. Six missed calls from a blocked number. He called Miriam, reassuring her they were okay and giving her the condensed version of what made them take so long to check in.

Zoe was better with people than any other person he knew. She moved to the bow of the boat and lay on her back, likely contemplating what had just happened down there. He opened the box that held the phone and took out some drinks. He crawled up and lay next to her. The waves rocked them as the sun warmed and dried.

Distant sounds of laughter and hoots of successful dives carried on around them, but they were alone. Alone on their boat island for some well-needed R & R.

"How is she?" Zoe asked, referring to Miriam.

"Spooked that we didn't call. She's starting to act motherly."

Zoe lifted her brows. "Which is creepy since she was dating my brother."

A small moment of silence followed her light mention of Seth. It was the first flippant comment he could remember about him since...well...since he went missing. "You were amazing down there."

She didn't deny it but didn't agree either.

A look of deep concentration came over her face. She rotated and sat, crossing her legs and facing him. "Thank you for this," she said and gestured to the water around them. "But it's not Australia. I'm keeping you from what you love. From what you want."

Frustrated, he sat and faced her. "Babe." He looked from one of her eyes to the other, searching for something. He wasn't sure what. Taking both of her hands between one of his, he reached in his pocket. "You are what I love. You are what I want."

He took the ring and held it out to her. "I want to love you forever. I want to share a home with you. I want you to have our children. I want you to say you'll marry me."

"I can't breathe." Tears ran freely down her flushed cheeks. She shook her hands like she'd just burned them. But she wasn't holding out any fingers and certainly not the one on her left hand.

"Will you marry me?" he said, no longer relieved.

"Yes," she said and tackled him to the fiberglass, nearly making him drop the ring. Her lips were soft and eager, and they were his. Forever. He pushed the cowboy hat from her wet hair and laced the fingers from his free hand through the waves of blonde. Only Zoe Clearwater would forget about the ring, he thought, as fervent lips found his and strong arms wrapped around his back.

He pushed away and lifted, propping himself on an elbow.

He held out the ring and turned his head, keeping his eyes on her expression.

The green sparkled as she studied it like a treasure unearthed from deep in the sand. Pointing to each of the smaller diamonds, she said, "These are you and I." Then, she tapped the larger stone in the middle. "This is us when we're together. Bigger. Stronger. It's beautiful. Thank you." Her tears dripped on the back of his hand as he slipped it on her finger.

He groaned and lowered himself over her.

"Other than the Tiki Bar, Show Me's is the only other place on the island with dancing," Zoe said to Raine. She didn't want to have an engagement announcement party without one of her sisters. And the Tiki Bar was out of the question. The owners had found a federal loophole and broke every turtle-safe law on the island. "Mom and Dad are coming. Come on. It's a Monday night, and we're meeting at eight. What else do you have to do?"

Raine sat on her heels in the sand, her knees resting on a towel. "Maybe I have a date."

Zoe let out a long laugh.

Since federal and state laws require nest excavations seven days after hatching, Raine had an arm nearly shoulder deep in the hole she'd dug. Since this was a green nest, the hole would need to go deeper yet. Zoe vowed to get her excavation and relocation permit this winter when Raine offered her courses for the island volunteers.

"All right, I'll go, but if Blake Eaton is there, I'm not making any promises about keeping my mouth shut."

"Dear sister, we wouldn't expect any less of you." There was good reason Raine was the way she was. She devoted her life to the conservation of a species only to pull in adults that had been drowned from fishing nets or ropes. She'd peeled hatchlings off the road from disorientations that took them inward toward illegal lighting. She'd saved grown turtles with boat propeller cuts so brutally deep, she didn't see how they survived. Often times, they didn't.

Zoe looked around as Raine pulled out the first dead hatchling. Yes. She knew why Raine was the way she was. It was hard to watch, so Zoe forced her gaze outward. The water was choppy, but it didn't seem to scare the children or the birds. The children rushed the waves, diving fearlessly into them. The birds ran in and out like the water was moving lava.

She could spot a local, and she could spot a tourist. She appreciated both. The former gave the island roots and TLC. The latter provided life to Ibis.

The man she spotted didn't fit either description. It wasn't Chief Roberts. She would recognize him even out of his uniform and uncharacteristically out of his office. The man wore new sandals much too expensive for trudging through the sand. His Bermuda shorts still held the seams from sitting folded on a shelf in a clothing store. Regardless, she rubbed the spot on her arm where Roberts had bruised her even though the mark was long gone.

"We've got a live one," Raine announced.

Sure enough, tenderly, Raine pulled out a tiny, squirming hatchling. She held it between its back and underside as its flippers tried to swim away in the air. Placing it in the box top Raine had prepared next to the nest, she reached in and found another. And another. Soon, she had five piles. Dead turtles, live ones, unfertilized eggs, shell fragments, and full shells for tallying data. All would be recorded on the nest's data page on her tablet and eventually reported to the state.

Soon, Zoe vowed. She would no longer be the only Clearwater sister who couldn't hold one of those little guys.

Matt sat at his desk staring at Zoe and Dane like he was analyzing them. He had yet to say anything other than empty introductions.

"You're engaged," he said as a statement, then glanced over his desk at her left hand.

So he could get a better view, she lifted her hand and wiggled her ring finger. "I don't wear the ring in public. We aren't seen together in public."

"Except Show Me's."

"We were the only ones in the parking lot that night."

"And Luciana's."

"We were the only ones in the entire bar. Are you worried someone else from Ibis might have been in the Florida Keys at the same time we were, too?"

"Yes."

Zoe sighed. Cops were thorough. "Why did you bring us here?"

"I'm moving Miriam."

Her shoulders fell. "Why?" It was a dumb question. He'd basically told her why, but she still couldn't believe it. She'd failed her. She was supposed to watch out for Miriam, for her brother's lover. And she failed?

Matt had already been painfully right once. He'd told her she may have wanted it to be murder. It might have been easier for Seth's disappearance to be solely someone else's fault rather than a diving accident that would have been prevented if she were with him. If someone wanted him dead, they would have done it with or without her. She wasn't about to let her conscience do anything like that to Seth again.

"If she's safer somewhere else, so be it."

"What?" Dane interrupted. "Who could possibly think she's

at my house? What would they find if they did? The blinds are all drawn, just as they've been for weeks, no, months."

"I have connections in Reno and Chicago. She'll be safe."

"Will you send her to Reno?" Zoe asked, knowing it was petty. "She would like Reno. But Chicago? No offense."

Matt shook his head but said, "I can probably have that arranged." He stood and held out his hand. "Congratulations on the engagement."

Dane shook with him before Matt held his hand out to her. He shook like a man, but Zoe was a Clearwater. She pulled him across his desk and gave him an a-frame hug.

Eli stood at the entrance to the bar section of Show Me's. He looked down at little Chloe and scowled.

"It's a party, Eli," Zoe begged. "We'll only be a short while."

"I can't let her in. You know that." He looked around, then leaned to Zoe's ear. "But if you go through the dining area and take some family pictures of the sunset, you might just end up in the bar from that side of the beach." He stood back up, stone-faced like a heartless bouncer.

The place was nearly empty. They were the first ones there from their group. Only a few small clusters of forty-plus men and women out for an early drink.

And Dane.

He sat with one hip on a bar stool, sipping from a bottle. He wore faded jeans with real shoes. His shirt was probably a size too small, and hugged the muscles in his shoulders. This was her man…her fiancé. It sent chills from her head to her toes. He winked as soon as he spotted her, lifting his bottle in an imaginary cheer.

Then he turned to Chloe. "Look who showed up to crash the

party," he said as he approached them. Chloe blushed. He called to the bartender and ordered her a ginger ale with a little paper umbrella.

They started trailing in. Her father, her mother, Willow. Liam came later with Raine close behind. The ring rested safely in the tiny pocket of her sundress. Tonight, she wore her cowboy hat out of celebration versus necessity.

They sat around the large group of tables Dane had already moved together. Her family sat on one side with the two of them on the other. He looked at the hands of each of her family members, Liam's, too. Checking their hands to see if they had drinks? He must have been satisfied because he curled his hand around her waist and lifted. It was firm and strong and took away any nerves that threatened to creep up her spine.

"Thank you for coming out tonight. We have an announcement," he said.

They'd discussed this. As a couple. As a team. Each set of eyes lifted toward them in unison. He dug his thumb and forefinger in the tiny pocket of her cotton dress. "I realize there's a lot going on right now, but I want you to be the first to know—well, first after Miriam who was sort of there—Zoe has agreed to marry me."

She had no idea if he had more to say. And it didn't matter since her family erupted in cheers so loud, they drowned out the music. Glasses were lifted and clanked. Everyone hugged everyone, including the men. You would think they'd won the Lotto. Each abandoned the cluster of tables and pulled one another out to dance in celebration. Her father with her mother, Liam with Chloe, Willow alone, much like she used to do around their childhood firepit, dancing to fictitious sand gods.

"This is the second best day of my life," Zoe said as his hips seduced her to the beat of island bongo drums and snares.

When the song finished, he dipped her dramatically and

kissed her long and hard. The silence was sudden. It took her a moment to escape the imaginary bubble she'd placed herself in with Dane. When she opened her eyes, Dane was looking toward the door. Stone-faced. Defiant. He pulled her up and twined his arms around her.

Moving her gaze in the direction of his, she spotted them standing in a line. The Sun Trips crew. In a quick head count, she thought it might have been every single one of them. Each of them staring at their embrace. And the ring that glittered in the dance lights.

"I told them to come," he said stoically without moving his glare from them. "Mandatory staff meeting over a few complimentary beers."

Zoe nearly fell over herself as she straightened her dress. The same looks ensued, Greg looked to Lilly elbowing her in the ribs as he leaned over to gossip in her ear. In fact, each one of them seemed to hold some sort of silent communication.

It was the damnedest thing. Before she could lift her hands in an effort to explain, the group lifted their arms and cheered louder than her family. Her eyes darted to Dane's, his to hers. Rounds of firm pats on the back and shoulders followed congratulations and comments of, "It's about time, man."

She could hardly get her mouth to open, let alone speak any coherent words. Relief flooded her. Closure fulfilled her. It was a good night. A great night.

TWENTY-SIX

Slightly buzzed from the alcohol and much buzzed from the turn of events, Zoe let Dane dig her keys out of her tiny purse much the same way he did the ring from her pocket. The ring. She lifted it and watched it sparkle in the moonlight.

"Where will we live?" she asked as he unlocked the door. "Do you think your parents will make it all the way back for the wedding? The wedding. When should we—"

He turned the knob and let them tumble through the door. Narrowly, they missed the coffee table and landed on her plush carpet. He pressed his hips into hers, making her forget homes and dates. His lips were tender, yet needy. They left a line of warmth as they traveled along her jaw, down the center of her neck. He took the spaghetti strap from her shoulder and pulled it down leaving her sexy and exposed. Her heart sped. Her breathing spiked. His hands, his glorious hands molded and explored, leaving her a puddle of want.

She lifted his shirt over his head as she wrapped her feet around his waist, pulling him closer to her, heat to heat. He wanted her. He pulled the straps the rest of the way from her arms, then lifted her hands above her head. She lay there with the soft at her back and hard pressing against her front. He moved his hands over her like he was discovering her for the first time. Would it always feel like the first time with him?

Her back arched, reaching for him. Inviting him. She tried to unfasten his pants, but he took her wrists and shook his head. "Tonight, you're mine." She could have exploded just from the three little words. A cool breeze wafted over her skin as he pulled her dress to her navel, leaving a moist trail from his tongue in its wake.

He lifted the bottom half of her dress, grasping her above it, cupping her below. Kissing her everywhere as if his life depended on it. Her body shook, then bucked. She erupted in his hand, her shoulders pressing into the floor. She knew her hands were supposed to stay above her head. She told them to stay there, but they seemed to have minds of their own. She had to touch him, feel him. All this damned material. It probably seemed like a small tantrum, but she maneuvered from beneath him, removing their clothing piece by piece and tossing it somewhere she didn't know.

Dipping her body against his, she crawled up his abs, over his chest and landed at his mouth. It was her turn to grasp and tease. The growl that came from deep in his throat only encouraged her until he grabbed her wrist with more force than he had when he tossed them both to the floor. Pulling her head back, she tried for the most evil yet sensual grin she could muster.

The next growl came from deeper in his throat. She found herself flopped on her back with muscled hips between her thighs. He paused long enough for protection before leaning low and looking from one of her eyes to the other. She didn't know what he was looking for, but he must have found it because he sunk into her painfully slow, then stopped. Her body shook. Her hands dug into his sides. She could feel her eyes blur, lose focus then rekindle as she lifted her hips. He followed much like he did when they danced, leading sensually, never missing a movement. The beat of their dance quickened, her head moving from side to side. He lifted as they moved together, holding out his hands. She laced her fingers in his. He held tight, keeping her grounded. He always kept her grounded. Kept her focused.

The focus was bliss. It was love. It was real. And it exploded with a force that could shake the calmest of waters. "Now," she screamed but he was already there. Always there. They pressed, arched, and dug in for the last push, then again.

The sudden weight and warmth of his body made her realize how desperately she'd been breathing. Her chest moved up and down against him as his did the same. She was acutely aware of their racing heartbeats as, they too, danced together. Quickly, then slower, until their sweat-slicked bodies lay lifeless and spent. Her joints were gloriously unhinged, her muscles fatigued. She wouldn't leave this spot. They would order out food and let the delivery people toss it next to their naked bodies.

"I want to marry you just as soon as you will let me," he said into her hair. "My parents will come. And I will live wherever there is you."

Headed for the grocery store, Zoe turned the corner out of her driveway as she spotted a piece of paper folded in half and left on her dash. Dane. How did this happen? Her happiness was clouded with the lack of closure of Seth's murder. No, that was negative. Her mother would take out the incense, darken the room, and make Zoe meditate until she changed her thought pattern. Instead, Zoe pulled over and decided to do that without the meditation.

Dane was what made this all bearable. He would be there for

her in easier times and in hard. The note was a chicken-scribble drawing of a set of pots and pans with a small arrow showing where she could find them in his kitchen. He was moving in. Officially. Her heart couldn't fit much more.

The grocery store could wait. She headed toward the north end of the island and turned up the radio, letting the wind whip her hair under her hat and around her face. *I will live wherever there is you.* Her hand lifted and covered her mouth. Beneath, she smiled from ear to ear. She loved her little house, but he wanted children. She wanted children. They hadn't discussed how many, but a two bedroom house wouldn't be big enough. She knew she was getting ahead of herself, but Dane's house was bigger. It needed loads of work, but the lot was large, a rare find on Ibis. His drive wound back a few hundred feet with large towering trees on both sides. She stopped halfway down, imagining a swing hanging from one of the branches.

She parked and walked up to the front door. Lifting the empty planter next to the door, she used the spare key and stepped in. She flicked on the light just inside, her eyes landing almost immediately in the center of the room.

Miriam Roberts. She sat facing Zoe, tied to a chair. Her mouth was covered in duct tape and one of her eyes was purple and swollen shut. She was shaking her head furiously, her good eye blood shot and terrified.

Behind Zoe, the door slammed, making her jump and spin around where she stood.

Police Chief Roberts blocked her exit.

Dane stuck the card he bought Zoe in his glove box. On it, he'd written some stuff he thought she would like. He talked Raine into giving her a three-part course so she could get the sea turtle conservation certifications she'd been wanting. He had to bribe Willow with an offer of free babysitting so Willow would cover for Raine and free her up to give the classes. It was worth it. He found a loving-our-engagement card. They made cards for everything. In the envelope, he stuffed the paper Raine gave him with the time and place for the classes.

He'd called three times. She was probably in the shower, but they had an agreement. As long as all this crazy shit was going on, they would answer their phones. Three times was enough. He was going over there.

On his way, he'd used his hands-free to call Harmony. She was happy to hear from him, even happier he was joining the family, but hadn't heard from Zoe. Same with Raine and Willow. Hell, he even called Osborne and left a message.

When her house was empty, he tried to keep himself from overreacting. Too damned late.

He sped to Sun Trips, then Willow's restaurant, even the grocery store she'd said she was stopping at. When his phone rang, he nearly dropped it out of his Jeep trying to answer.

Caller ID wasn't Zoe. "Yo," he yelled.

"It's Osborne. I got your message. I triangulated her phone. She's at your place."

He could do that? "Shit, man. I'm sorry. Just jumpy, I guess. Thanks for checking it out. And…you can do that? That's some creepy shit."

He heard Osborne laugh on the other end. "We're getting closer, Dane. Watch your back."

He knew Osborne was cryptic for a reason, but it reassured him nonetheless. Disconnecting, he did a careful three-point turn.

Zoe's wrists hurt. Her face hurt. Her ankles. But she knew she didn't look anything like Miriam. Zoe was duct taped to a chair around her ankles, her hands behind her back. Just as Miriam was. Across her mouth was a long piece of duct tape that stuck to her ear on one side and in her hair on the other.

Chief Roberts paced the floor, ranting. "You did this, you little bitch," he screamed as he stopped in front of Miriam. "I told you I'd kill you if you tried to leave me. You're mine." He ducked his face close to hers as he shook.

The difference between hearing those words from the chief and hearing them from Dane was profoundly different. Dane. Would she ever see him again? He hadn't drawn the picture of pots and pans. She'd been an idiot.

He wouldn't come out here. They hadn't been here in days. Funny, how the tears wouldn't come. They were going to die. The chief was pacing, waving his arms, and promising it over and over again. Then, like a complete lunatic, he squatted down next to Miriam and brushed the hair from the crusty blood on the side of her face. "I loved you." He said it like he was a prize catch and she was losing him to another woman.

Carefully, he walked outside and shut the door gently. Within seconds, Zoe heard splashing. On one side of the house, then the back. An overwhelming smell of gasoline crept into her nostrils. Oh no. No, no, no, no. She jerked her gaze to Miriam. Tears dripped out of the eye that wasn't swollen shut. Zoe swore they weren't selfish tears.

With the sound of a loud whoosh, the house shook. Flames erupted, then crawled over the window panes like the rising tide. They were going to burn.

Dane was relieved that Greg was on for the afternoon cruise. As a bonus, the guy said he was cool with his engagement to Zoe. In fact, nearly the whole staff was. Of course, they thought he and Zoe had been engaged for months. Didn't matter anyway. Like it or not, he was the boss. He didn't care. She was going to marry him and be his forever.

As he turned onto his drive, he saw smoke, then a flicker. A random pain clenched his gut. He pressed the gas harder and swerved down the drive. Flames. Flames crawled up his house around each side. Please, no. Her Jeep was in front. Somewhere inside his head he noticed the police car, but all he could focus on was Zoe's Jeep and the flames. He turned off the engine before he came to a complete stop, pulled the brake and jumped out. The gravel slowed him down as he made a straight line for the front door. Not Zoe. Not his Zoe.

Ready to kick the front door through the flames, he made it close enough to feel the heat before he was clotheslined and landed flat on his back. Through the stars, he saw Chief Roberts. The pointed end of a cowboy boot landed square on the side of his rib cage, narrowly missing his solar plexus.

She was in there.

"You'll never prove anything," Roberts yelled as he reared back a fist. "I was called to the scene of a fire."

Dane rolled, dodging the fist that came at his face. He kicked out his feet, taking Roberts' down with them. Dane scurried to straddle him as Roberts fell with a thud.

"And now I can add assaulting a police officer," Roberts said with an easy grin.

Dane didn't care about anything but her. He grabbed Roberts' uniform and landed a full-force punch to the side of his face. Then, another. And another. He didn't stop until Roberts lay unmoving.

Zoe.

Grabbing his injured side, Dane ran toward the front door

before holding up his free arm at the heat. He couldn't get close enough to kick the door. Darting his eyes over the condition of his house, he decided on the back.

He ran to Zoe's Jeep and grabbed the blanket she kept in her survival gear. Tossing it over his head, he ran around the side of his house, yelling her name as he went. Whether it was going to work or not, he tossed the blanket over his head, ran for the back door, and hit it with his shoulder.

The door crumbled beneath him, and he fell to the floor. Please be alive. The smoke was thinner down here, so he crawled along the floor. The closer he got to the center of the house, the fewer flames there were. He looked up and saw them licking the ceiling, threatening to take everything down.

She was there. In his living room. She lay on her side on the floor, strapped to a chair with duct tape covering her mouth. Her beautiful green eyes stared at him with a fear he could not have imagined.

The relief was instant, but it mixed with panic and confusion. She was alive. He moved his arms and legs as fast as they would scurry across the floor, then pulled the tape from her face.

"Miriam!" she yelled. "Get her. She didn't tip her chair. Her face is up in the smoke."

He whirled to see Miriam Roberts tied in the same way Zoe had been. Her head dangled to one side.

A piece of ceiling collapsed near the front of the house making Zoe scream. Zoe? Or Miriam? Or both?

His eyes burned in the smoke, his heart in the moment. Coughing, he looked around for something to cut the tape. He rolled to the desk drawer and grabbed his envelope opener. Slicing the tape, he freed Zoe first. He grabbed her face, her arms, checking each part to see if she was still whole.

"Take Miriam. I'm okay," Zoe yelled as she coughed and started crawling toward the back door. He released Miriam's limp body from the chair and slung her over his back, following Zoe. Sparks flew and mini explosions rushed flames around them. Heat threatened his extremities, and he doubted any of them would make it.

He'd never been so glad to reach the stuffy, Florida summer air. As they rolled out into it, the sound of roaring flames was replaced with sirens. Pushing Miriam carefully next to him, he crawled to Zoe in the dirt and pulled her on top of him. The feel of her body. Her arms as they grabbed hold of him. He ground his teeth together and did everything he could to keep his head.

Loud cracks and the sounds of building materials crumbling to the ground were mixed with the whoosh of spraying water. Men in full firefighter gear came around the side of his house, yelling over their shoulders when they spotted the three of them.

The heat and smoke still burned his eyes. The men were foggy, but he watched them as he held Zoe tight. A figure came from around the dude in front.

Roberts.

Dane's head fell back and thumped on the ground.

"Arrest these three," he heard Roberts yell.

Dane rolled his head to the firefighters who looked to each other. Ignoring the chief, they asked Dane, "Is there anyone else in the house?"

Zoe answered in a raspy squeak. "No one. Chief Roberts kidnapped me and this woman."

"I said arrest these people," Roberts screamed, pushing the firefighter who asked the questions. "Arrest them, or I'll have your jobs."

"We're firefighters, sir," he said, coming to his feet. "There's a fire."

As the chief screamed profanities around them, a firefighter checked Miriam for vitals. She was alive. The firefighter talked in a walkie to someone about her condition.

"Can you walk?" the other one asked him and Zoe.

"I'll arrest these two myself—"

"Chief Roberts, you're under arrest for the murder of Seth Clearwater." It was Osborne. He spoke with a hand on his gun, walking in low, one arm outstretched in front of him, palm up. "You have the right to remain silent…"

Dane collapsed on the ground, pulling Zoe in tighter.

"Um, sir," It was the firefighter. Dane thought. Maybe.

He could hear Roberts going ape shit, Osborne ordering him around. Dane didn't care. He had his Zoe.

"We'd like to get some oxygen on you two," said a voice near him. "I will bring it back here for you."

Dane kissed the top of Zoe's head. Her hair reeked of smoke, but he could still smell his Zoe. "We can walk," he said. They rose slowly, and he noticed Osborne taking Roberts away in cuffs. Too bad Miriam couldn't see it. They were loading her on a stretcher.

Dane's drive looked like a used car lot for the city. Police cars, marked and unmarked, fire engines, ambulances.

Purposely, he walked close enough to hear the conversation between Roberts, Osborne, and another officer. Roberts demanding the reason for his arrest. Osborne responding with something about a witness who swears Roberts told him he was going to kill Miriam's lover. About Roberts threatening to strangle a man he thought looked at his wife the wrong way. Something about a plane ticket to Reno in the chief's name tagging him as a flight risk. Osborne told him to forget about bail with the amount of money they found in his bank accounts. A police chief with that kind of money?

It was hard not to stare. Roberts turned more shades of red than Dane knew existed. "I have connections," Roberts howled. "I'll have each of your badges before this is over, and it's far from over." Spit flew as he yelled. Osborne put a hand on Roberts' head and guided him into the back of his car. If only Dane had a camera.

Zoe stood fifty feet from the shore. The sun was just setting. It mixed with scattered clouds creating brilliant oranges, yellows, and blues. They were mirrored in the waves that rolled in and out like a waltz.

"Here you go, little sister," Raine said as she lifted the bucket Zoe had kept in her shower throughout the day. It was covered in a towel, but Zoe could hear the dozens of tiny flippers scraping the sides. One hundred twenty-six sets of tiny flippers sensed the cooling evening air. They were from a daytime hatching and had been collected by the now-certified Zoe.

Rarely did any of the Clearwater family miss a hatchling release. They kneeled in two tight lines between Zoe and the water. Dane was between Willow and Harmony.

Tourists began to wander over, curious, hoping the gathering had something to do with sea turtles. Tonight, they hit the jackpot.

Certified and legal—thanks to Dane—Zoe took the towel from over the bucket. Inside was a mass of commotion, little guys and girls letting instinct move them.

"Come on over." Zoe used her free hand to wave at the tourists. "We're about to release a nest of hatchlings. You're welcome to join either line, but please watch your movements as the turtles make their way to the water." She checked carefully to make sure everyone was still, providing an adequate path for the hatchlings.

"A nest of hatchlings emerged this morning," she began to explain. As Raine's class had taught her, she picked one up, pinching it gently between its shell and underside, then held it up.

The crowd let out a chorus of oohs and aahs, her family included. "They emerged in daylight which is a dangerous time for hatchlings. The birds and fish that are their predators would easily see them. Since only about one in a thousand of these little guys will survive to adulthood, regulations say we capture them, release them in the dark and give them a fighting chance."

She set the bucket in the sand in front of her. "The hatchlings need to make this walk to the water and feel the sand beneath their bodies. It's part of the process of survival. Please stay put as they make their way." Carefully, she tipped her bucket. And the race was on. One hundred twenty-six turtles each about the size of a silver dollar ran across the sand between the line of human knees. Instinct provided a powerful driving force and led them in a straight line to the water.

"Don't touch them, please," Zoe said as she monitored the spectators carefully. "If you notice one that needs some help, a certified volunteer will give it some assistance." A few stragglers took their time or wandered in the wrong direction. Since they represented much of the last two years of Zoe's life, she picked them up and turned them toward the horizon, prodding them on.

It was much like what Dane had done for her.

The first few reached the shore and were kicked back by the tide. It was as if the water forced them to prove their worthiness by fighting. And fight they did. Rushing back and forth with the coming and going of the waves, the turtles kept moving until they disappeared in the dark liquid.

―――――――――

It was a party. Most people wouldn't understand, but that was okay. Rarely did people understand Zoe's family. Judging from the turnout at Seth's funeral, people were okay with not understanding. Go figure. The Sun Trips employees, too. Almost all accepted her relationship with Dane and her role in the business.

He'd put Willow in charge of the flowers. Zoe noted she chose daisies and carnations instead of the calla lilies and roses at Seth's traditional funeral. They were in every corner of the pontoon boat as well as hanging from the awning. A large bowl of daisy petals rested at the bow of the boat.

The noise of celebration drowned any hint of wind or boats passing by. The girls wore sundresses with flat sandals. The guys had on linen shirts and pants. It was hot even for an early August day coasting on the Florida Gulf. No one minded.

The boat bobbed in the choppy water as Liam drove. He played music about *Banana Pancakes* and people that were *Better Together*. Willow and Chloe stood next to him.

"They're idiots."

Zoe felt the cool breeze from his breath and inhaled the scent of leather and ocean.

Dane.

Giving herself ample time to recover from the sudden blast of sensory overload, she asked, "Who?"

He gestured his head toward Liam and Willow. "Blind idiots."

Ah. "It's complicated."

"Not really."

He turned to face her and placed the palm of his hand on her cheek. "You…are complicated. This…" He lifted her hand and rolled her engagement ring in a circle. "…is not." Bringing her hand to his lips, he kissed the ring before dropping his mouth to hers.

"Get a room." It was Raine, of course.

It made her laugh as she realized the boat was slowing down. Liam chose a spot near The Kitchen. The birds from the sanctuary eyed them wearily. Her family stood and all took their places around the perimeter of the boat. Everyone was there. Her mother had strong-armed Matt and Miriam to join them as well.

Liam set the anchor and Harmony stepped forward in the circle. "We are here as a Celebration of Life for the time we had with Seth. Those of us who would like to, please share something you're thankful for and a wish you have for Seth or his legacy. I'll start by thanking him for the times he kept Henry and me together. It was hard to work in the day and go to school at night, raising a child as a teenager. But it was harder not to smile when he took his first steps or said his first words. My wish is that he is smiling at this celebration right now from somewhere above." She took a handful of daisy petals and threw them down wind. A gust grabbed them, scattering the white petals in a playful dance before landing in the water.

"I want to thank Seth," Raine said as she took a step into the center of the circle, "for not ratting me out the times he caught me underage at the Tiki Bar."

Their mother grinned and added, "My Stitch and Bitch friends told me about those times, dear. You were in college. I kept an eye on you."

"Stitch and Bitch?" Dane huffed in Zoe's ear. "I adore that woman."

In fact, it took a few minutes before everyone stopped laughing.

"I hope his legacy carries on," Raine continued. "Through Luciana's bar, the playful search for her dowry and the attraction it brings, keeping this island alive."

Each took their turns. Some were serious. Most were humorous. Chloe thanked Seth for his version of how babies were born and hoped grandma wouldn't tell her any more of that stuff. When everyone had their turn, Zoe's mother faced Miriam and Matt. They glanced to each other before Miriam spit something out in her napkin. Zoe assumed it was nicotine gum. "Seth saved my life in more ways than one. On so many levels, I was wrong to be with him. I'll never forget him and am so very sorry for what my husband took from me…from all of you."

Tears began streaming down her cheeks. Matt saved her by speaking up. "I want to thank you all for your help in the investigation. I can say that, right?…and I hope I can do justice for him by putting away the person who did this."

Matt's eyes darted around from person to person. Zoe noticed him inhale before holding up both hands. Her father let out a rare, "Whoot!" and ordered Liam to turn up the music.

Zoe took Dane's hands and wrapped them around her back, moving her hips in a figure eight as she pressed them into him. Raine walked by with the bowl of flower petals. Dane rotated him and Zoe so they could watch as she held it out to Matt. He seemed to sigh with relief. Reaching in, he grabbed a handful and threw them up in the air. Everyone lifted their hands and turned the boat into a dance floor.

They drank and danced and ate, then danced some more. These were her family and friends. And her treasure hunter. He dipped her low as he pulled her thigh around his solid hip and kissed her hard. Hers forever.

The music was loud and a small feast was eaten. Miriam sat alone, watching the water as they trolled along the coast.

"I have to ask," Zoe said as she lowered into the chair next to her. "I understand why you broke into my parents' home, even my place. But why Seth's apartment building? Did you think the letters could have been in the walls of his place?"

Her eyes were red as they turned to her, but the tears weren't falling. She looked honestly puzzled. "Someone was looking in the walls of Seth's apartment?"

ISLAND PURSUIT

THE ISLAND ESCAPE SERIES, BOOK 2

It killed Liam to see her like this. Doing her Yoga thing with one arm. She sat on the floor with her legs out, cradling her bad arm like a newborn baby. Willow Clearwater wasn't the type to complain. With a straight back, she slowly leaned forward until her bad arm nearly touched the floor in front of her. Damn it if it wasn't sexy.

Leaning against the doorjamb watching her was probably boarder line creepy, but his head was a mess since the attack on her parent's restaurant. The overhang to the outdoor patio had been fixed days ago, yet Willow would be in pain with a useless arm for weeks to come.

As he watched, he realized her long blonde locks were flatter than usual. "Why don't you let me wash your hair for you?"

She didn't jump at the announcement of his presence, but her body stilled. Her back gently expanded, then contracted as she rose to an upright position. When her eyes turned to meet his, the blue was warm and inviting. Beautiful tiny lines radiated from the corners as she smiled. "Liam. Hello. You would do that for me?"

He sighed. Of course he would. "I would."

She crisscrossed her legs then stood, unfolding herself like a smooth, human accordion. "I set up some stuff in the kitchen. I was going to try and do it one-armed after I got some kinks out."

"You shouldn't have any kinks." He could feel the heat of frustration radiating up his back.

She stood and made circles with her good shoulder. "You have kinks of your own. How is your back?"

He headed toward the kitchen to see about this 'stuff' she had set up. "It's nothing."

"Holding up an extensive wooden overhang isn't *nothing*. Have you been doing the stretches I showed you?"

He didn't turn but heard her melodic voice following him. "Yes." The stretches had helped. It was amazing. He felt nearly healed while Willow had a useless arm and shoulder.

As he turned, she unzipped then removed her yoga jacket using her good arm. His heart jumped into his throat, choking off any form of air. Beneath was one of those sports bras that came below the ribs. Her smooth lanky arms draped the jacket over a chair. The dumbfounded look on his face must have been apparent since she finished her stroll to the sink with her arms crossed over her chest.

He was still frozen when she stopped at the sink and looked over her shoulder in question. Her long, blonde hair partially covered her face causing his feet to begin to walk purposefully toward her in order to brush it behind her back.

Smiling meekly, she turned to the sink. "Are you sure about this?"

Reaching over her, he turned on the water. She smelled like the flowers her mother planted in the planter boxes on her porch. He took a towel from next to the sink and folded it in front of her. Gently, he placed his hand on the back of her head as she lowered over the ceramic bowl. Using the hand spray, he waited for the water to warm while stroking the long locks of her hair to one side. She turned her head, exposing the lids that closed over her beautiful blue eyes.

He stepped closer, pressing along the backs of her thighs as he ran the warmth over her scalp. Her body melted into him as her hair ran wet over his hands. Careful not to compromise her shoulder, he turned off the water and found which bottle read, 'shampoo.'"

"Why didn't you ask someone to help you with this? You have two sisters." And you have me. You will always have me. He poured some shampoo into the palm of his hand, considered how much hair she had, then poured some more. He used his fingertips to spread the silky bubbles over her scalp. Massaging, cleaning. He could get lost in this woman.

The muscles in her back relaxed and he swore he heard a small croon come from her lips. He quickly rotated away from her as his body reacted as it always did when he was close to Willow. How long could he go on like this?

Available in Paperback and eBook at Your Favorite Online Retailer or Bookstore

ALSO BY R.T. WOLFE

The Island Escape Series

Island Secrets

Island Pursuit

Island Reveal

The Nickie Savage Series

Savage Echoes

Savage Rendezvous

Savage Deception

Savage Disclosure

Savage Betrayal

Savage Alliance

The Black Creek Series

Black Creek Burning

Flying in Shadows

Dark Vengeance

ABOUT THE AUTHOR

R.T. was born and raised in the beautiful Midwest, the youngest of six ornery children. She married at a young age and began her family shortly after. With three amazing small boys, life was a whirlwind of flipping houses and working two jobs in between swim lessons and Candyland. Now that her boys are nearly grown, R.T. spends much of her time writing and on the road traveling from one sporting event to another serving as mom and cheerleader. She works to assist several non-profit organizations that have supported her books and to promote the work they do for those who cannot help themselves.

WWW.RTWOLFE.COM

facebook.com/rtwolfe2012

twitter.com/rt_wolfe